"Let's not worry about town gossip!"

Sighing, the old lady continued. "I don't think there's anything that would help."

"I think I have the answer," Joel interrupted. "Madeleine and I will get married. Won't that solve the problem?"

The words hit Maddie's mind like a nuclear bomb going off. Of all the improbable gifts on her Christmas wish list, there was nothing she wanted more than that! And still—

"You can't do that," Madeleine protested. "My reputation isn't that important."

"On the contrary, your reputation and your aunt's *are* that important. Furthermore, since I'm the cause of the problem, I should be the *solution* to the problem. I'd be happy to marry you, Madeleine."

"For Tante's sake?" she muttered, half in protest.

"No—for all our sakes." Joel insisted.

EMMA GOLDRICK describes herself as a grandmother first and an author second. She was born and raised in Puerto Rico where she met her husband, a career military man from Massachusetts. His postings took them all over the world, which often led to mishaps—such as the Christmas they arrived in Germany before their furniture. Emma uses the places she's been as backgrounds for her books, but just in case she runs short of settings, this prolific author and her husband are always making new travel plans.

Books by Emma Goldrick

EMMA GOLDRICK

madeleine's marriage

Harlequin Books

TORONTO • NEW YORK • LONDON
AMSTERDAM • PARIS • SYDNEY • HAMBURG
STOCKHOLM • ATHENS • TOKYO • MILAN

Harlequin Presents first edition October 1989
ISBN 0-373-11208-4

Original hardcover edition published in 1988
by Mills & Boon Limited

CHAPTER ONE

THERE WERE eight warped wooden stairs leading up to the back porch of the house next door, a twin to her own house. Two identical Steamboat Gothic mansions not a hundred feet apart, the remembrances of the turn of the century in Laconia, New Hampshire. Madeleine went up those stairs in the darkness two at a time, head down, heart pumping angrily as the Heavy Metal din rose another twenty decibels. It was hardly a problem. Madeleine Charbonneau was a great deal of girl, standing five foot ten in her stockinged feet, weighing in at a svelte one hundred and forty-four pounds.

So when her bowed head landed squarely in the stomach of the watcher on the veranda, he gave a muffled gasp and fell backwards in a sitting position. And because *he* was six feet three and built like a football line-backer she landed all askew in his lap, the hem of her full skirt floating somewhere around mid-thigh, and her head in a whirl.

'Well, look at what I've caught!' The baritone voice was almost in her ear as one of his arms came around her and locked on. 'And what kind of bird are you, love?'

Maddie saved her breath for scrambling. Her karate lessons had not been for nothing. A quick twist, a push that sent him flat on his back, and a jump, and she was on her feet, glaring down at him, her sudden fear turning instantly to anger.

He hadn't even dropped his cigarette. The end glowed for a moment in the darkness as he took a puff, and then he was up with all the agility of an athlete. Maddie dropped into a defensive crouch, both hands poised for a chop at him.

'Hey, wait——' The cigarette-end glowed again, and a low-pitched chuckle followed. 'I'll give it up. Honestly!' The little burning tip circled in the air expressively as the butt was snapped out in a wide arc to fall into the dew-damp grass.

Madeleine, her head still in a dither from the impact, pulled herself up to her full height, barely able to concentrate. The miracle of it all was that his voice came from above her. A woman who had spent half her life slouching so as not to insult some male ego could hardly help but be surprised. She struggled mightily to force her mind back into the proper channels. 'Give what up?' she spluttered indignantly. It wasn't the question she had meant to ask, the words just popped out.

'Smoking,' he returned solemnly. 'A filthy habit, let me tell you. But tonight is my night for giving up things. A change of direction in life, so to speak. Besides, I'd rather give it up than have you chop me with those lethal hands. Look at the *size* of you!'

Unable to see him clearly in the moonlight, or to understand him at all, she let the gambit pass. 'I wasn't *about* to chop you,' she told him stiffly. 'I *never* go around chopping people—without good cause. It's just that—well, the party is very annoyingly loud, you know. And my aunt is eighty-five years old and needs her sleep. This neighbourhood was *noted* for being the quietest area in New Hampshire!'

'Was it really?' A gusty sigh whistled out of his massive chest. He almost sounds as if he regrets it, Maddie thought. But how could that be? He's one of the crowd. As Grandpa used to say, if it howls like a wolf, bites like a wolf, travels in a wolf pack, it's a wolf!

She fell back an uneasy half-step as he came closer. In the pale summer moonlight she perceived the vague outline of a tuxedo—white ruffled shirt-front, black tie, black jacket, and above all this, some five or six inches above her eyes, a mass of blond hair, cut short but standing in unruly disregard of the hair-styles. There was a magnetic something about him that seized on her heart and left her a little flustered.

'I—my aunt Marie—she's very old,' she stuttered. 'She can't sleep with all the noise, and I can't work! Do you know who——?'

'Who's giving the party?' Another dry chuckle out of the darkness. 'Joel Fairmont is his name. Made a mistake, did he? Anybody with a wild party in mind should have sense enough to invite all the neighbours so they wouldn't call in the law.'

'You know this Mr Fairmont?'

'Like a brother.' He grinned, and in the dark she could see the sparkle of a perfect set of teeth. 'Not that I go around admitting that in public, you know.'

'I could see why you wouldn't,' she sighed. For the moment all her anger had run out, leaving her—confused. 'But I have to make a protest—for my aunt's sake, you understand. What sort of a man is he?'

'Sort of a man?' he mused. 'That's hard to say. A Boston playboy. Maybe that tells you something. Money—loads of money. Not that *he* ever made a nickel by himself, you understand. How about you?'

'About me what?'

'What do you do? Doctor? Lawyer? Interior decorator? Schoolteacher?'

'None of the above,' Maddie said wryly. 'I'm a real-estate salesperson. Er—where do you think I could find him?'

'A real-estate salesperson? Great!' If he were being sarcastic Madeleine couldn't tell. His voice was still as sleek as a snake-oil salesman's. 'He's around somewhere,' he responded, taking another step closer. 'I'm glad you never.'

'Never?' Maddie's head was settling down, but she was still confused. The conversation was completely escaping her. Have I fallen into a madhouse? she asked herself. And if so, is this the prime inmate? A straggle of moonbeam, late for the party, caught up with his face. Smooth, young, unlined, with a square chin. Eyes wide apart, their colour unknowable in the silver light. The blond hair was silvered too, becoming almost white, falling down in one unruly lock over his right eye. And a tiny smile played at the corners of his mouth.

Precognition splashed a warning signal through Maddie's mind. I know you, her conscience screamed. From some other life, some other time, I know you!

'Never,' he chuckled. 'I'm glad you never chop people——'

'Without good reason,' she added defiantly. There was a sudden need to be defiant. Some faint warning in the back of her mind. This man is a caged tiger, rattling at the bars! Take care, Madeleine Charbonneau!

'As you say,' he chuckled. 'I always had trouble with that.'

'How terrible,' she snapped, her anger breaking through again. The world had been irritating her all day, and now this party, this man, seemed to be the focus of all her petty little hatreds. 'Now what about Mr Fairmont?' It came out as cold as spring water in North Canada.

He ignored the chill, which only added to her irritation. 'I always had trouble because I'm so big,' he mused. 'All the way from Middle School, kids would gang up on me. And my mother would say *force is not the answer!* Ha! What did she know about living in Lilliput?' For a moment he stretched. Maddie could almost *feel* those muscles rippling under his shirt. 'Go ahead,' he concluded.

'Dear God,' she snapped, 'I'm a fairly intelligent woman. I have a college degree. I go to church regularly—well, almost regularly. I speak three languages. Why don't I understand you? Are you—sloshed?'

'No, I'm not sloshed. Pleasantly high, perhaps, but certainly not sloshed. Go ahead.'

'In about thirty seconds, if you don't get out of my way,' she snapped, 'I'm going to forget my upbringing and hit you!'

'That's it!' A big grin spread across his mobile face, putting the moon to blush. 'Now you've got the right idea, girl. Go ahead.'

'Go ahead and what? Hit you?' Maddie shifted uneasily. She was a big girl. He was a bigger man. He fairly loomed over her. And despite the fact that she jogged regularly and exercised twice a week, hitting people was not her favourite occupation. But if he insisted——

'Go ahead, hit me,' he chuckled, slipping out of his jacket. He dropped the garment unceremoniously over the porch rail and flexed his arm muscles.

'So all right,' she muttered, clenching her teeth. 'You asked for it!' At least it might help relieve some of *my* frustrations, she thought. As she weighed the situation, he brought both open hands up in a typical karate defence. So I won't use karate, she told herself. Her right hand knotted into a tight fist and she swung away at him in a roundhouse hook aimed at the side of his jaw.

Drunk or sober, dark or light, his response startled her. Instead of backing away or lifting a hand to block her, he took one large step forward until his starched shirt-front dimpled her round full breasts.

Her right hand, instead of bouncing smartly off his chin, missed entirely and wound up harmlessly encircling his neck. At the same time one of his arms locked around her midriff while the other arrived somehow at the nape of her neck. 'See?' he murmured in her ear.

She was too startled to move, or even to respond. The physical contact brought more sensations than she could handle. Perhaps it was the beauty of the night, or the long, tiring day, or the conjunction of her stars, she thought as she desperately tried to command some movement from her own muscles.

'And then, if it were a girl,' he continued calmly, 'and she wanted to fight back, I would——'

'I'm not fighting,' she interjected, gasping. 'Please. I'm not fighting!'

'Too late,' he whispered. 'It's all reflex action.' Maddie opened her mouth to protest, but his lips had already found the target, sealing in whatever words she might have mustered. There was a heady mixture of tastes on his lips, none of which she could identify, but the thought of 'tastes' lingered, even as other impressions pressed in on her nerve centres.

There was a surge of excitement, starting deep down in her stomach and flooding all her being. There was a whisper of caution that stood out for a second, and then was blotted out. There were fiery reports—like nothing she had ever felt before—as he pressed her close. So close that they were touching from lips to thighs, and every touch fed its own little flame. She hung in his arms, unable to command her own knees to support her.

When he broke it off she continued for a moment to rest on his strength while she fought for breath. She opened her eyes turgidly. *He* was having some breathing problems too. It was the tiny little thought that kicked her own body-machine back into operation. As the power of his arms slackened she pushed herself away to stand unsteadily on her feet. One hand reached behind her for support from the porch rail. They stared at each other for a moment, silent.

'Well!' He finally broke the silence with all the quiet interest of a scholar. 'I've never had *that* response before!'

'And you never will again,' Maddie growled at him, working hard to build up her armour of anger again. 'I came over here to make a perfectly polite complaint, and you—you *assaulted* me!'

'I have to confess I enjoyed it too.' There was a certain amount of exuberance in his voice; the arrogant signal of male conquest that Maddie hated so much. She wanted so badly to puncture his little balloon.

'It reminded me of something,' she said in a mild little voice. 'When I was eight years old a cow licked my face,' she went on grimly. 'I think you and the cow must have come from the same school.'

His eyebrows arched in astonishment. 'Have I lost my touch?' he asked. 'After all these years of girl-watching, have I come unglued?'

'No. No! Wait a——' she started to protest as he gathered her up in his arms again and tried another sample. With the same results. Madeleine stumbled back against the porch rail when he released her, her hand scrubbing at her trembling mouth. What are you doing? her conscience shrieked at her. Getting ready to bow down and kiss his foot? The man is dangerous!

'Was that better?' he asked anxiously. 'Or perhaps you'd prefer a different sort of sample?'

'No—I—don't bother,' she stammered, edging away from him. 'I can—see that you must have been very successful when you were young.' He took a step in her direction. 'You still are, I suppose,' she added shrilly.

The moon came out in full glory at just that moment, reflecting a very self-satisfied expression on his face. 'I always like to have satisfied customers,' he observed.

Maddie might have said something cutting. Certainly there were a dozen or more words of that nature on the tip of her tongue, but her world was too full of moonlight and dreams. She was so excited, so fascinated, that unheralded tears began to roll down her cheeks. He tucked an index finger under her chin and coaxed her head up. Maddie took a quick shallow breath and stared.

'I think—I'd better get about my business with Mr Fairmont,' she gasped. She reached up to pat her hair back into place—a useless procedure; it lay the way it wanted. She could brush and comb and pin it to a fare-thee-well, and within minutes it would return to its own original condition.

'Lovely hair,' he said softly, reaching out his index finger to touch it gently.

'You don't even know what colour it is,' Maddie grumbled awkwardly. He grinned at her, and moved his finger farther.

'Fishing for compliments?'

'No, of course not,' she said indignantly, and was thankful for the cover of night, that hid her blush. She *had* been fishing, and could not understand why!

'Silky brown hair,' he announced in awe, lifting a lock up above her head. It might well have been in the same tone that Columbus used when he first sighted the New World. Maddie shivered with pleasure, but the gold of it turned to instant dross. 'Why do you need Joel?' he asked. 'I can do anything he can—and better.' There was a one-sided smile on his face, and his hands were reaching for her again.

'No!' she exclaimed, backing farther away. 'Mr Fairmont? Where would he be?'

He shrugged his shoulders. 'Beats me, lady.' Maddie turned on her heel and stalked into the house, leaving him alone in the moonlight. And just to prove how dependable his word is, she told herself, he's lighting up another cigarette!

Once inside the house the noise smashed at her ears. Someone was playing a stereo system at full blast. As Maddie rested her hand on the kitchen wall she could feel it shake under the impulse of the heavy bass tones. More than a little courage was required for her to open the kitchen door and step out into the living-room.

There were perhaps twenty couples crowded into the double parlour. *Couples* might have been the wrong word. There were two distinct groups. One was un-shaven, long-haired, clothed in worn jeans. The other was a dinner-jacket crowd, complete with neckties. With one marvellous exception. At the foot of the mahogany staircase a woman posed, her head artfully concealed under a tremendous lampshade—and wearing not another stitch. A bearded young man was on his knees in front of her painting a scenic sunset on her rounded stomach, with her navel serving as the sun. It was all being done with considerable panache, and it was not a bad painting at all.

Maddie sidled by that pair carefully. Laconia was not far from Boston in road miles, but a considerable dis-tance in social graces. The roar of conversation, all pro-duced at maximum level to override the stereo, was positively doing ear damage. Not knowing whom to ap-proach, she worked her way to the centre of the room and then did a slow turn, looking for some island of sensibility. It appeared in the form of an older man—perhaps in his forties—sporting suit and tie and two glasses of something. He was a tall, bulky man, who moved with purpose.

'Here you are, darling,' he shouted at her, handing over one of the glasses. She took it, smiling, and made a toasting gesture before she sipped. For the first time that night she relaxed. The man was friendly; he might even be mentally stable!

Whatever it was in the glass must have been com-pounded with formaldehyde. Maddie choked, reached for a handkerchief to dry her eyes, and handed back the glass.

'Not to your taste?' the man yelled. She shook her head and coughed to clear her throat. A woman passed by with two glasses of a clear sparkling something in her hand. Too proud to beg, but not to steal, Maddie snatched at one of them. It turned out to be American champagne, slightly warm. When she looked back to her interrogator she could manage to speak.

'My great-aunt,' she shouted at him. 'Sleeping!' She pointed out of the window in the direction of her own house.

He answered just at one of those poorly defined moments when the stereo player stopped to change records, and all the conversationalists stopped to listen. Into that vacuum he bawled, 'No, I won't sleep with your aunt. I told the agency to send you!'

He grabbed her wrist and started to tow her towards the stairs, amid cheers from the now-interested audience. Madeleine dragged her feet.

'I think you've got the wrong idea,' she protested. A chorus of comments from the watchers proposed plenty of unorthodox suggestions. Some were so far out that Maddie blushed, stamped her feet, and forced the procession to a halt.

'Look,' the man complained to her, 'I've already paid the agency bill, so there's no need to pad your part.'

'Turn me loose or I'll call the cops,' Maddie grated desperately through clenched teeth.

'Dear lord,' the man towing her grumbled. 'You *are* over sixteen, aren't you?' He reached over to tweak her breast with a clammy hand, testing the product, so to speak. And Maddie exploded. In one swirling movement she locked on to his wrist, turned away from him, and

when he lunged in her direction, used his movement and
her leverage to throw him over her hip.

He crashed into one of the conversation groups like
a bowling ball in a ten-pin alley. Conversations splattered in one direction, and people in the other. The cheers
turned to screams as couples scrambled to get out of the
way. The big man got up groggily off the floor, spotted
his adversary, and headed in her direction.

Maddie did a quick search of the room and located
the stereo system, an expensive and complicated model
standing in a corner on a series of racks. When the man
came at her again, both arms spread to envelop her, she
let his momentum push her backwards as she locked on
to his shirt-front, fell backwards to the floor, seated both
her feet in his stomach as they fell, and, while rolling,
catapulted him halfway across the room and into the
stereo set. The big machine continued for about ten
seconds, then began to slow, and finally the music died
in a wail of anguish. The man lay in the ruins of the
music, waving his arms feebly.

There's only one more thing required, Maddie thought
quickly. An evacuation programme. Into the babble of
confusion she shouted, 'The cops! The place is being
raided!'

If she had yelled 'Fire!' there could not have been a
speedier reaction. In this host of partygoers there seemed
to be a very large number of guilty consciences. A con-
certed rush for the door began. Which was why, when
the man from the porch wandered in, Madeleine
Charbonneau was the only guest left in the house.

'What happened to my party?' he asked in a peevish
voice. His words were not quite as smooth as one might
expect. He surveyed the wreckage of the room with a

rueful look on his face. 'Looks like a hurricane hit,' he muttered.

'I—I'm sorry about that,' she said. 'Look, I'll help clean it up. When Mr Fairmont shows up I'll—good God!' She ducked her head as some flying thing whirred around it. 'Bats!' she screamed. A childhood fear, that. The fear that a bat would fly by and entangle its tiny feet in her hair—and the hair would all have to be cut off.

'No bats around here,' he commented. She took another look at him, wondering if her eyes had not gone out of focus. Sitting on his left shoulder was a bird. The two sets of fore-and-aft toes gripped his coat. An orange stomach, green wings, yellow head, eyes outlined in white, and a huge beak. Her mind grappled with it. And the parrot fluttered its wings, turned one eye on her and squawked, 'Lookit the lovely knockers!'

'Good lord!' Maddie said in astonishment. The bird ducked his head under his wing and muttered 'Pieces of six' in an outraged voice.

'Isn't that supposed to be ''Pieces of eight''?' Maddie asked, strictly in the interests of educational research. 'Long John Silver, and that sort of thing?'

'How would I know?' the man grumbled. 'Bluebeard was my grandfather's parrot. My grandmother hated them both, so she sabotaged the bird's schooling process. Where did everyone go?'

'I don't know,' Maddie murmured innocently. 'I told them about my poor old aunt—and all the noise and stuff—and darned if they didn't all get up and leave. Of course there was some talk about a raid. By the narcs, I think. Maybe you'd better go yourself?'

'Narcs?' he queried, puzzled.

'Yeah. The narcotic police, you know.'

He stopped to consider that, and a grin formed on his well-knit face. 'Well, I can't go,' he said clearly. 'I live here!'

'You what?' Maddie echoed in disgust, and measured to see how far he might bounce if she applied another hip-toss. 'You're Joel Fairmont?' He returned a somewhat vacuous smile that was close enough to a confession for Maddie's angry mind.

The man had spent considerable time pumping her full of misinformation, and he deserved everything that was coming to him! The only trouble was that he didn't quite co-operate. When she manoeuvred him into position for the fall, instead of following her movement he planted both feet and called a halt to the procedure by wrapping both arms around her and hanging on.

'You're either a very stable drunk, or you're putting on a good act,' she snapped as she tried to wriggle out of his hold. Strangely enough, that sour smell of heavy drinking had faded from his breath. It was all very confusing, and Maddie was tired.

'Maybe both,' he agreed equably. 'Oh, and I think I should mention, during my *wanderjahr* I spent several months as a professional wrestler. Hold still. Gee, lady, you sure know how to put a damper on a party!'

'I told you before,' she said bitterly, 'my aunt needs her rest, so I shut the party down. I've done you a big favour, Mr Fairmont. You can't just pile your Flatland friends in here and let them run wild all night. You're lucky I didn't call my uncle Fred.'

'All right,' he replied sarcastically, 'I'll bite. Who is your uncle Fred?'

'He happens to be the chief of police in this city,' she informed him happily. 'He worries about Tante and me, living all alone the way we do.'

'I can see you really *are* a spoilsport,' he grumbled. 'I don't want to meet your uncle. This party was my last and final fling, lady, before I stick my nose to the grindstone. You've been in on the decline and fall of the last of Boston's only clear-channel playboy.'

'Grindstone?' She was unable to hold back the question.

'I'm writing a book,' he snapped. 'It takes quiet and concentration, right? So I throw a going-away party, get all the noise out of my system, and now I'm ready to get to work.'

It *had* to be true, Maddie laughed to herself. He sounds so darn mournful about it all. This wasn't a party, it was a wake! No wonder he had hidden out on the porch. As for his friends, as far as *she* was concerned, the parrot was the only one who talked sense in the whole house!

'Don't take it so hard,' she comforted. 'You wouldn't be so maudlin if you weren't so drunk.'

His head came up. Blue eyes, she noted almost automatically. A perfect match for that slinky blond hair. 'Drunk I'm not,' he declared casually. 'But I will be. Talk to me about four in the morning when I'm *really* drunk, and you'll see the difference.'

Maddie eased carefully past him. A man who declared his intentions that way was sure to be a problem. 'I think I'll go now,' she said. 'Thanks for reducing the noise-level.'

'Yes, of course.' He waved a hand vaguely to dismiss her thanks, and then had another thought. 'Hell,' he snapped, 'I don't even know your name!'

'Charbonneau,' she offered, backing away from him as he stretched. 'Miss Charbonneau.' There really wasn't enough backing room left in the wreckage of a room. Without moving an inch he had her pinned up against an overturned maplewood table, and her plan of escape flew right up the chimney.

'Miss Cochembeau,' he muttered. 'Well, what would you expect for a name way up here in the mountains? Come over here.'

It wasn't a command upon which she had to make a decision. He didn't wait for that, but locked five fingers on each of her shoulders and pulled her hard against him.

'Charbonneau,' she corrected frantically. It was the last clear thought she was to have in this long dark night. He kissed her.

It has to be because I'm so tired, she told herself dreamily. Because everyone knows there's no such thing as love at first sight! She offered a token resistance and then let it all happen. Warm rising feelings from the pit of her stomach chased little sparks up her backbone. Her pulse rate began to climb far beyond the danger signal. Her head began to dissolve into instant pudding as his hands wandered up and down her back.

The whole scene might well have had a bedroom ending, but his parrot, agitated by the whole procedure, zoomed down on the pair of them, settled on Maddie's shoulder, and nipped her ear with that sharp beak. The pain shook her back into sensibility just in time. She froze, and Joel Fairmont, feeling the change, slowly released her.

'I *am* losing my touch,' he murmured mournfully. 'The little bird has flown.'

'You'd better believe it,' she replied disdainfully. 'Now and for ever.' She continued to struggle, but although he held her loosely there was no escape. 'Turn me loose!' she hissed.

'Why don't we have a nightcap and settle our differences?' he suggested smoothly as he released her. Maddie shrugged herself down, ran a hand through her hair, and adjusted the neck of her blouse. By judicious scanning of the room he located the only plate of hors d'oeuvre left untouched, and presented it.

'Have a nibble,' he suggested. 'It will settle your stomach.' She looked quickly down at the plate, fearful that in the short space her eyes were away from his face he would think of something drastic to do—like kissing her again.

'No, thank you,' she said. 'I'm careful what I put in my stomach.'

'What *have* I got here?' he mused. 'One of the original Puritans? Surely one little drink wouldn't ruin your life. And we *are* neighbours, right?'

A thought ran through her mind, and became an instant full-blown plan. There was nothing Joel Fairmont needed more than a good old-fashioned set-down. And I'm the girl to do it, she told herself.

'I don't know about that,' she said demurely. 'I don't drink a great deal.' Conniving, that's what Tante Marie would say if she could have known. 'But perhaps a nice tall, cool beer?'

He grinned at her. She could almost see the gears turning over in the back of his eyes. One late night plus one large beer plus one large girl means—all is not yet lost!

He was still grinning when he came back out of the kitchen with two large beer mugs in hand, and passed her one. The beer looked perfect. Beads of moisture clustered on the outside, and the tiny white head seemed just right. He offered her a toast. They clinked mugs, and Maddie made a great performance out of looking down.

'Unlucky,' she told him, pointing down to his shoe. 'Toasting with an unlaced shoe is unlucky. That's an old French Canadian saying.'

'Is it really?' he asked as he bent his head to look.

'Indeed it is. Would I lie to you?' She started to laugh, and was unable to stop as she poured her entire glass of cold liquid over his head.

'What the hell!' he roared.

'Pieces of six,' his parrot squawked.

Joel Fairmont straightened up slowly. Madeleine backed away carefully until she bumped into the frame of the front door. His eyes had lost that sparkle that called to her so much. And there was nothing sensual about that cold chill that ran down her spine. Fear, un-adulterated fear, it was!

'Lady, you *are* a party-pooper, aren't you,' he stated in a cold grim voice. 'Well now, just do me a favour.' His voice rose a decibel or two. 'Get out of my house. Get off my land. Get out of my life!'

Maddie turned and ran for her life, out of the front door into the darkness, through the grove of maple trees, across the moon-striped lawn that separated their two identical houses, and through her own back door. She slammed it behind her and leaned against it, out of breath, and out of courage.

Mehitabel, her aunt's big white tomcat, vaulted up to the top of the kitchen table and watched her, his greying head swinging slightly back and forth as his shining eyes tracked her movements. She whirled around and set the bolts, then leaned her head against the door to catch her breath. After a moment she moved like an automaton across the floor and out to her little office, where she slumped into one of the straight-backed chairs next to her desk.

Her hand shuffled through the pile of paper at which she had been working when the party noise had brought her steaming out of the house and up the little hill. Her hand found the pencil she had dropped, but her mind did not seem to recognise it. Joel Fairmont's picture ran up and down, side to side, across her eyeballs. Two hours earlier she hadn't even known he existed, and now——?

'God,' she muttered, 'get out of my life!' Of all the things she had seen and heard that night, his last command was one thing she could not comply with. She remembered that flash of precognition that had smashed through her mind when the moonlight first illuminated his face. Intuition? Remembrance? Or perhaps just spring fever, come a month too late?

A big-city, arrogant womaniser, she told herself. A thoroughly objectionable man with thoroughly objectionable friends. Why couldn't it have been some nice, quiet, elderly scholar who had bought the house next door? But the memory of his kisses clung to her longer than she would like. She tried to brush away the memory by scrubbing her lips, and accomplished nothing.

Mehitabel came into the tiny converted office and rubbed against Maddie's leg. She abandoned all hope

of doing any of the hundreds of pieces of paperwork
that lay before her. Selling real estate in the house-hungry
Lake district of New Hampshire was easy—until you
were faced with the mounds of paperwork that must accompany each sale. Every one of those papers piled up
in front of her were due yesterday, but she could not
handle them. A restless hand pushed them aside as her
mind switched.

'I know you, Joel Fairmont,' she muttered as one
perfect tear formed in her eye. 'I must be some kind of
twenty-seven-year-old idiot. It ought to be easier to fall
in love with some nice man than some horror like that
man. Luckily there's no such thing as love at first sight.
But if I want to survive *this* man I'm going to have to
keep away from him. Far away!'

It was a thought that tried—but failed—to comfort
her all night long.

CHAPTER TWO

MORNING NOISES. The chatter of sparrows outside her window. The harsh call of gulls, fishing the lakeshore. The excited squeal of a child over on the little beach at Opechee Park just behind the house. And a rattle of dishes in the kitchen, the room below her bedroom.

Madeleine stretched luxuriously, her mind only gradually coming back on line. It had been a wild evening, even if you balanced out all the pros and cons. And during the night she had been through one of the most excruciating dreams she had ever dreamed. She sat up in bed, looked at the twisted sheet, the pillows on the floor, and the crumpled condition of the lace at the throat of her shortie nightgown.

A night to remember? Or one to forget! What a thing to dream about. Long John Silver, with his parrot riding one shoulder, his eye-patch pushed up on his forehead, where it mingled with a loose lock of fair hair! What was the expression? Having his way with her?

The kettle whistled from the kitchen. Second alarm, Maddie told herself ruefully. Even on Saturday Tante Marie ran a taut ship. But those thoughts dissipated the wild image haunting the back of her mind. 'I know you, Joel Fairmont.' She pronounced the words in a sort of incantation, hopped out of bed, and promptly forgot him. The bathroom mirror reflected the same imperfections she had mourned for years—a bridge of freckles across her tiny nose, the pale scar above her right

eyebrow, a memento of the night when her team won
the Women's Basketball Championship of the state of
New Hampshire, and a straying elbow had knocked her
into the spectator seats. A tiny chip missing from her
left upper canine, a memorial to her High School softball
career.

Maddie was still grumbling as she slipped into her
running suit. Bright crimson, with gold stripes down the
sides of her shorts, and a fluorescent 'X' on the back
of her jacket, to give warning to motorists when she went
jogging in the dangerous twilight. The suit fitted her like
a soft glove, caressing every full curve, marking every
limit, doing the best it could, she reminded herself, to
disguise the sheer size of her.

She offered the mirror a little moue of disgust, and
ran for the stairs just before Tante Marie stuck her head
around the corner of the kitchen door and shouted for
her.

Maddie paused for a second at the door. It was hard
for her to describe Tante Marie. A short spare creature,
whose thin white hair barely covered the bald spot in
the middle of her head. A quietly appreciative woman,
except on one subject. The lady who, at the family conference after the funeral of Maddie's father and mother,
had voluntarily assumed the care of the two-year-old girl,
and who had never turned back. A woman who, after
her eightieth birthday, accepted the driving energy of the
woman Madeleine had become—accepting her man-
agement diffidently. Except in one area.

'Ha! You run again?' Tante Marie wrinkled her button
nose as she busied herself around the kitchen. It was the
same argument Madeleine had heard every morning for

the past ten years, and it ran to its inevitable conclusion. 'Such a thing to wear outside!'

'It's perfectly respectable,' Maddie murmured as she sidled towards the back door.

'Respectable,' her aunt sighed resignedly. 'Dresses are respectable. And that terrible noise last night! I could almost blow my head!'

Maddie grinned. It was about as unladylike an expression as one might ever hear from a great-aunt. 'Blow your stack,' she corrected automatically.

'Head—stack—who could ever understand this language!' The little old lady, shuffling around in her slippers, was barely five feet tall. She hated the fact that her great-niece was so much taller, and could look down squarely on that bald spot. It was a measure of the old woman's despair when her voice shifted from gentle to shrill, her veined hand running through her thin white hair. Eighty-five years old, Tante Marie Tetrault still insisted that her trip from French Canada, begun over seventy-five years earlier, was only a temporary visit.

But this was one morning when Maddie knew just exactly what would short-circuit the discussion. 'I went next door last night to complain,' she hurried to squeeze in. 'Our new neighbour is a young man!'

Tante Marie stopped dead in her tracks. 'A *young* man? Is he married?' The important question of the day, in any discussion with her aunt, Maddie knew.

'I forgot to ask,' she admitted ruefully. Her aunt threw up her hands in discouragement.

'Drink your orange juice,' Tante Marie directed. 'You forgot? This modern generation! All the wrong people are having babies! Drink!'

'It's not good to run on a full stomach,' Maddie insisted. 'You wouldn't want me to get cramp, would you?'

'What I want is you should get married,' her aunt snapped. 'Children we should have around the house, *non*? What happens when you went over there last night?'

'I—well, they were making too much noise. I asked them to stop, and they did.'

'And what about this man?' The aristocratic nose went up in the air. Total disbelief absorbed some of the hundred wrinkles on her tiny old face. And then Madeleine's boundless need to cheer the old woman overflowed, and she put her foot firmly in her mouth.

'Well,' she started off cautiously, 'he certainly is— handsome, well-spoken. But arrogant! Lord, he thinks he's the most wonderful person in the world!'

'Yes, of course,' her aunt sighed with a coolness that splashed ice over Maddie's fire. 'Since you are fourteen, girl, once a year, as regular as the seasons, you meet the most wonderful man in the world and fall in love at first sight. How about that? Are you married? Are there children in the house?'

'Oh, Tante,' Maddie mourned. 'Not that bad. Surely not that many!'

'How many times?' her aunt grumbled. 'Once we are almost at the altar, *non*? I liked that Alfred. What does he do now?'

'He's a big success,' Maddie confessed in a pained voice. 'He's a garbage collector, head of his own truck crew.'

'And he married someone else?' her aunt prodded.

'Yes,' Maddie admitted. 'He married the O'Brien girl. You remember, the little redhead who was the cheerleader? I've hated redheads ever since. They have seven— or maybe it was eight—children.'

'Ha—a narrow escape,' said Tante Marie, smacking her lips. 'Four is enough. The Bible says "Go forth and multiply", but it doesn't say you have to do it all by yourself. Seven children is boasting. And that boy George? When you were twenty-one?'

Maddie blushed fire red. 'It turned out that he wanted a great many things,' she stammered, 'but marriage wasn't one of them.'

'Buttering me up,' Tante Marie nodded sagely. 'I thought so at the time. I can tell that kind from ten miles away. But I tell you, Madeleine, every time you come charging in to talk about Wonderfulman or Perfectman or Intellectman, what happens? No, you don't tell me— I tell you. Just as soon as the first blush wears off they all turn out to be milk-toast men, *non*? So never mind Perfect—just tell me, does this man have guts? A mind of his own? What you need is a man with a strong hand, *chérie*.'

'I don't need *any* sort of man,' Maddie insisted. 'I'm perfectly happy the way I am. You and I—that's enough for me!'

'Nonsense,' Tante Marie interrupted. 'So is he another—what do they say today—a wimp?'

'No—not *this* man,' Maddie protested. 'I couldn't— no.'

'So, all right,' Tante Marie continued. 'This one is too much man for you. So forget him. Go out and run hard. Get lots of exercise. Keep busy. Pretty soon your brain will not be so swollen up, and things will be normal again. Now, is that everything?'

No, he's not too much man for me, Maddie wanted to protest. He's the wrong *kind* of man for me. But the protest died on her lips. Tante Marie, despite her image, was too fragile for deep argument. So change the subject!

'That's *about* all,' Maddie sighed, then grinned a wicked teasing grin as she looked up at her great-aunt. 'I met this Mr Fairmont, and I found out his terrible secret!'

'Did you really!' Tante's eyes lit up. 'Tell me, quick. He is a bank robber? The bridge club comes this afternoon.' The old woman was actually licking her lips, Maddie noted. And sipping at *my* orange juice!

'Why, it's really very simple,' Maddie teased, pushing her chair back. 'He writes books and keeps a parrot!'

'Just a minute,' her aunt wailed. 'You can't leave it like that! And you didn't drink your orange juice!'

'I must have,' chuckled Maddie. 'My glass is empty. I have to go, dear. I'll tell you more about it when I do my total laps.'

She went out into the morning, laughing, but what her aunt had said nagged at her. Could it be true about her choice of men? Try as she might, she could only recall four, and none of them very clearly. Am I such a bad judge? Maddie asked herself as she trotted solemnly down the veranda stairs. Deep in the recesses of her mind a seed of doubt had been planted.

Mehitabel met her, as always, at the foot of the stairs, and trailed her half-way across the lawn until the cat displayed considerably more sense than his mistress, and lay down in the shade of the only oak tree on the property. A breeze was blowing out of the north, laden with moisture from its passage over Lake Winnipesauki,

New Hampshire's largest body of water. High in the sky overhead a broadwing hawk was soaring, hunting. The two identical houses rested in the shade of their trees. The brick and glass school, the only other occupant of this last block of McGrath Street, was silent, almost as if someone had slipped a dustcover over it for the twelve-week summer vacation period.

Madeleine took several deep breaths to pump herself up, and started off across the grass of her back garden towards the boundary of the little park. There was no fence to separate garden from park. Indeed, the only boundary was established by the fact that the city used a different sort of grass in the park. Nevertheless, in keeping with a childhood superstition, Maddie vaulted across the boundary and headed for the cinder running track.

The park was almost empty. The beach had not opened until eight—or as soon as the lifeguard arrived. And nobody else in the neighbourhood suffered from the terminal ignorance that drove joggers, Maddie told herself as she straightened her shoulders, checked her stopwatch, and started out.

There was no mileage marker on the track. A runner selected a spot to begin at, and counted for herself. In Maddie's case she always established her starting line at the base of the tall wooden carving of the Abneki Indian chief, set to face out on North Main Street.

By her tenth circuit she was blowing, reaching for second breath. By her fifteenth she had settled down in the interminable drudgery, and was suddenly not alone. A crumpled figure occupied one of the benches not ten feet from the statue. It was dressed to run, but obviously incapable of the act. Its head was tilted back at an almost impossible angle, and it was either dead or sleeping. A yellow-headed parrot was parading back and forth on the top bar of the back rest, clucking to itself, and occasionally reprimanding the man.

Madeleine slowed to a jog-in-place rhythm to examine the situation. 'Awk! Pretty baby!' the parrot shrieked. The man came to life with a start.

'Don't *do* that!' he snapped at the parrot, then held his head with both hands, as if his own voice had been too loud.

Maddie came to a halt. Almost anything would be worthy of attention in place of another five times around the track. She ran both hands through her hair to get it out of her eyes, pulled the sweatband off her forehead, and did her best to be super-cheerful. 'Good morning, Mr Farmont,' she called.

He peered up at her from the slot between two of his fingers. 'Fairmont,' he groaned. 'Do you always have to talk so loudly? Can't you see I'm ill? You wouldn't happen to be a doctor, I don't suppose?'

'No, I don't suppose so,' she returned cheerily as she found sitting room on the bench, but on the opposite side from the parrot. 'Hung-over, are we?'

'Bring aft the rum, Darby,' the parrot squawked. Joel Fairmont winced, trying to cover his ears and his eyes, with only two hands to work with.

'Why me?' he muttered. 'I came out here to do a good deed, and everyone picks on me! Why me?'

'My, aren't we feeling sorry for ourselves?' Maddie offered, not the least bit sympathetic. Although she was able to accept the theory that alcoholism was a disease, she found it absolutely unbelievable that a hangover should be cozened. 'Maybe you should go back to bed and die? Or would you prefer that I leave you alone?'

'No, not that,' he groaned. 'I made all this effort just because of you, and I won't have the nerve to do it again some other time.'

'How interesting,' she returned disdainfully. 'Did you know that you—and your parrot—are about to become the talk of the town?'

'Oh God,' he muttered. 'That's all I need! I chose Laconia because nobody knew me up here.'

'Well, that will be corrected by four o'clock this afternoon,' Maddie continued relentlessly. 'My aunt's bridge club meets then. By tomorrow at this time all Laconia will know. Now, just why would you want to find me this morning?'

He winced again, and shut both eyes as the sun came out from behind a cloud. 'I have a suspicion,' he said warily, 'that I might have said something last night that was—perhaps—a little out of line?'

'Several somethings,' she agreed affably.

'Well—then I'm sorry,' he muttered. 'I apologise.'

'And proudly said,' she told him. 'Your mother certainly taught you good manners. You must tell her I approve.'

'I can't,' he grunted. 'She hasn't spoken to me for two years. Doesn't that make you feel a little sympathetic?'

'Pity, yes,' she told him. 'But not a bit of sympathy. You really were a most disgustingly arrogant man last night.'

'That bad, huh?' He managed to get his head up, and his face clear of his hand. A pale wan face, a forehead wrinkled as if it were a plum on its way to become a

prune. And what happened to Handsome Harry?
Maddie asked herself, trying her best to stamp down on
both her laughter—and her growing sympathy. Is this
the arrogant male who haunted my dreams last night?
Unshaven, hair uncombed, he looked more like a rag
picker than a philanderer. If a police cruiser had come
by at just that moment, she decided, they would first
look for the wine bottle in the plain brown paper sack,
and then they'd probably arrest him for desecrating the
Peter Toth Indian statue.

But then, she thought, if you're going to love a man,
you have to take him warts and all! It took something
of the order of five seconds for her to realise what she
had been thinking. She gasped, and her hands covered
her mouth to be sure no words came out. *If you're going
to love a man?* Dear God, what's the matter with me!
An arrogant, bumbling, hung-over tramp? And I'm
going to love him? Am I for ever to be looking for the
bird with the broken wing? Madeleine gave herself a
shake, and tried to suppress the whole idea.

'Yes, it was that bad,' she confirmed. 'You're probably
not any girl's idea of Sir Galahad.' Except mine, she
added thoughtfully to herself, and I'm a certified lunatic
when it comes to evaluating men! Maybe that's why he's
so much better than—well, Henri, for example.

'Please,' he pleaded, raising both hands up in the air
in surrender. His parrot took flight, squalling in indignation, coming to rest on the prominent nose of the
Abneki war-chief.

'You don't *have* to do that,' he muttered. 'I came down
here at the break of day because I thought you were a
nice girl who deserved an apology, and now I'm not all
that sure.'

'I *am* a nice girl. Very nice.' She grinned at him, but
his eyes were on the ground. 'This apology,' she continued facetiously. 'Am I supposed to believe that you
no longer forbid me your house and your land and your
life?'

He looked at her, thunderstruck. 'Don't get the wrong
idea,' he said gruffly. 'I *meant* every bit of that statement
last night. The last thing in the world I need is to have
the neighbourhood snoop peering into my life. No, I
was apologising for the *way* I said it, not *what* I said.
What is that monstrous thing my parrot is roosting on?'
He shaded his eyes with one hand and tried to whistle
the bird down.

'Neighbourhood snoop, huh?' Maddie gave him a
speculative look, hiding the distaste that roiled in her
stomach. Her romance had started and finished within
five minutes on a park bench! The shortest record of
them all! Tante was right!

Madeleine had known a hundred men or more whom
she didn't like, but this was the first male to look beyond
her obvious feminine attractions, and admit he didn't
like *her*. It was another shock to add to the long train
of shocks, beginning the previous night! Neighbourhood snoop, indeed!

Maybe Tante was right about that as well as everything else. Maybe he was afraid of snooping, because
he had something to hide! So what I'll do, she told herself
coldly, is to *be* a snoop, and then spread it all over the
Laconia newspaper. If it's a fight you want, Mr
Fairmont, it's a fight you'll get. As of this moment, it's
open warfare! Starting with a little subterfuge and
subversion!

'That's our Peter Toth statue,' she explained in a purposely shrill voice, driving the nails a little farther into
his head. 'Toth is an immigrant sculptor who vowed he
would carve a wooden statue—a wooden Indian—in
every state in the Union. I don't know how far he's
gotten, but ours here is number forty-nine. Isn't that
nice?'

'Yeah, nice,' he moaned, then snatched at shadows.
'Indians, that's what I need! Some old Indian remedy.
Surely an efficient little thing like you could whip up
some old Indian recipe that would help?'

It was the phrase that he used that gave her a start.
'Little thing.' For years Maddie had wanted to be a *little
thing*. So when he chose—or stumbled on—her
weakness, it took a moment or two for her to remember
that they were enemies. She quickly revamped her
strategy.

'I don't know of any old Indian remedies,' she offered
hesitantly. That lock of hair fell down over his eye, and
it bothered her. Without thinking she leaned over and
brushed it back for him. 'How about an old Canuck
remedy?'

'Canuck? What in the world is that?' he grumbled.
'Some other tribe?'

'It's the name old-line New Englanders called us
French-Canadians when we first came south into the
States,' she chuckled. 'They meant it to be derogatory,
but now we wave it like a banner!'

'I don't need a banner,' he groaned. 'I need a rescue.'

'Well, come on, then.' She stood up and tugged at
him. His considerable bulk was not all that easy to get
in motion, but when he finally condescended to help,
the pair of them meandered down the cinder track like

an accident looking for a place to happen. Bluebeard, seeing them move, fluttered down to join the procession, choosing to perch on Madeleine's shoulder instead of Joel's. The bird had nothing to say, but its cocked head and glaring eyes indicated a deep interest in the changing circumstances.

Tante Marie must have been watching them through the window. She was standing on the porch holding the kitchen door open as they made their way up the broad steps to the veranda. Mehitabel was with her. The cat spotted the bird, sprang to the porch rail, then crouched, trying to figure a way to get to Maddie's shoulder.

The bird took two nervous steps back and forth, chattered aimlessly, and then croaked 'Pretty baby' as he launched himself and went fluttering away into the kitchen. Mehitabel spat out a frustrated yowl, and followed the same path.

'Oh, my God,' Madeleine murmured.

'Oh, my head!' Joel groaned.

'Oh, my!' said Tante Marie as she abandoned the people-pair and went chasing after the cat. By the time Maddie assisted Joel into the kitchen, a sort of equilibrium had been established in the animal kingdom. The parrot was perched high on the curtain rod above the window. The cat sat on the floor directly beneath, crouched ready to pounce. And Tante Marie, having measured Joel's condition with one quick look, was busy at some concoction, mixing half a dozen ingredients into one glass.

'Sit the poor man down at the table,' her aunt instructed Madeleine, and then in a sharp hiss, 'and then you get upstairs and put on something decent!'

There was no malice in Tante's words. She said it all with love—and from the background of her generation's values. Girls were born to be moulded; men had to be accepted as God made them.

Joel Fairmont was not the *first* man for whom she had mixed her concoction. Men were known to drink to excess. None of which, though, gave Tante Marie any sympathy for a drunk. Not at all. When she had finished stirring the tall, cool glass she handed it to him with a curt, no-nonsense, 'Drink every drop!'

He looked at it suspiciously. 'It's the same poison my mother used to make,' he muttered, holding the glass up to the light.

'Probably,' his tight-lipped hostess agreed. 'Every drop. You deserve it.'

'Damn the torpedoes!' the parrot roared at full strength. Mehitabel made a test-jump, got his claws into the curtain, and struggled to pull himself up. Age and the good life were against him. 'Haw, haw,' Bluebeard teased as the cat dropped back to the floor.

'Oh, shut up!' Joel snarled at the parrot as he sniffed the contents of the glass. His nose wrinkled in protest. 'I think I'm going to throw up,' he muttered.

'Drink!' The sweet old lady had turned into an elderly dragon. Joel tilted the glass full over, swallowed manfully, and almost choked himself to death.

'You'll be better in five minutes,' Tante Marie promised solemnly.

'Or dead,' he muttered. The old lady gave him a jaundiced look and was about to offer some more instruction to the younger generation, when Madeleine bounced back into the room and twirled for her great-aunt's inspection.

After her quick shower she had selected one of her most discreet outfits, the sort required when house-selling to middle-aged octopuses. A wide pleated grey skirt moved as she did. A classically simple white blouse, with lace ruffles down the front, gently caressed her full bosom. Restoring order to her light brown hair was impossible, but she had brushed it vigorously. Now it curled to her shoulders, and sparkled in reflected sunlight.

Her aunt paused in her busy programme and smiled. *'C'est magnifique,'* she said in admiration, then shifted gears to the practical. 'Sit. Eat.' She pulled Maddie's usually crowded breakfast plate out of the microwave and set it on the table in front of her. 'I forgot to tell you. Henri LeFleur called.'

'Oh, what did he want?'

'He didn't say. You don't suppose what he wants from you is something he would want to discuss with me? He keeps talking about cosy little cottages by the lake, just built for two, and then——'

'Tante!' Maddie snapped her head up. When Tante Marie started fencing with words she usually had all kinds of hidden motives. A quick look at the innocent face was enough to confirm that scheming was going on. 'Cosy cottages I don't mind, but he has other ideas, too——'

'Your boyfriend?' Joel Fairmont was glaring at her from across the table, as if half the world had just been destroyed and it was all *her* fault. There was no reason why she shouldn't tell him about Henri—but she had no intention of doing so.

'Not a boyfriend,' she returned coldly, thinking of all the trials and tribulations she experienced with her fifty-eight-year-old employer. 'It's a little difficult to think of a man of Henri's age and position as a boy!' And put *that* in your pipe and smoke it, *Mister* Fairmont!

His stomach must have been bothering him. He withdrew from the fray with another glare.

Breakfast was Maddie's main meal, and the only one that she allowed Tante Marie to make. The old woman was long past her prime, but not past her pride. She needed *something*—some usual routine—to keep her hands and mind busy. So the household compromised. Tante made the breakfast; Maddie laid out the light lunches, and dinners were a succession of casseroles or speciality dinners which Madeleine could prepare beforehand, allowing her to go out on her selling expeditions without tiring her aunt overmuch.

At the moment Maddie was simply not hungry, and would have pushed the plate aside, but Joel Fairmont, across the table from her, and trying unsuccessfully not to watch, was turning several interesting colours like yellow, green, and purple.

She picked up knife and fork, and started to work on the ham and eggs. 'You're not hungry, Mr Fairmont?' That lock of hair had fallen across his forehead again. Maddie watched gleefully while it swung gently over his eye.

'No, I'm not hungry, Miss Hochambeau,' he snapped, unconsciously pushing a hand through his hair. 'I never eat breakfast. Sometimes I don't eat lunch, either!' He tilted up his Roman nose in a 'so there' gesture. Maddie grinned back at him openly.

'Charbonneau,' Tante Marie corrected gently as she joined them at the table with one of her interminable cups of tea. 'It's a difficult name, and when my sister married——'

'Tante!' Maddie was half out of her chair, her eyes challenging her aunt to break off the story about the skeleton in the family history. For once the old lady refused the challenge, and held her silence.

'Strangely enough, I *am* feeling a little better,' Joel commented. 'Maybe I won't die today. So, if you ladies will excuse me, I'll make my way over to——'

'Pieces of six!' the parrot squawked as he zoomed down from the curtain and settled himself on Joel's shoulder. Mehitabel was up on the table top in one graceful spring belying his age, leaving a paw-print right in the middle of Maddie's sunny-side-up eggs, and knocking over her glass of milk.

'Oh, my!' Tante muttered as she tried to stem the tide of milk with only a paper towel. Joel rose quickly to his full height and put some distance between Bluebeard and the cat. Mehitabel snarled in fury, crouching with tail swaying slowly back and forth at the very edge of the table.

'I don't think your cat likes my bird,' he commented as he moved towards the kitchen door.

'On the contrary, I think Mehitabel likes your bird very much,' Maddie said coolly. 'In about the same way, Mr Fairmont, that I like you.'

He had evidently been restored to good health. His face lit up with a big grin. 'For dinner, you mean?' He was gone, and the door slammed behind him, before either of the women could think of anything to say.

Maddie, her meal already disturbed, walked over to the window and watched their neighbours stride across the grass between the two houses. Mehitabel joined her at the window, and her hand fell unconsciously to the scruff of his neck and scratched gently.

'There, you see?' she remarked to her great-aunt. 'There goes the neighbourhood.'

Tante Marie, hands full of milk-soaked paper towels, came over to join her at the window. 'Very much the man,' the old lady said in her pragmatic French-Canadian manner. 'Rough, with many sharp corners. Perhaps not house-broken, but then a good woman could do something with that, *non*?'

'Just a darn minute,' spluttered Maddie. 'If you're thinking what I think you're thinking——!'

'Why, I wasn't thinking a thing, love,' her aunt replied, going back to her rescue job at the kitchen table. 'Not a thing. But he *is* a fine figure of a man. So he drinks. What man doesn't have some bad habit? And I get the impression that he has a very sizeable bank account. Not true?'

'I—suppose so,' Maddie agreed. 'But——'

'But it should theoretically be just as easy to fall in love with a rich man as a poor one,' Tante Marie continued.

'Theoretically,' snorted Maddie. 'A woman would have to be brave or stupid—or both—to try it on with *that* man. He has an ego that approaches Biblical proportions!'

'Ah, but there are women—and there are women,' her aunt chuckled, as if the enigmatic expression explained itself.

'If you mean me, you've got the wrong woman,' Maddie said wryly, wrinkling her nose at the thought. 'And just standing here admiring his back won't get my sales reports finished, nor the house cleaned, will it?'

*   *   *

House-cleaning and shopping were two tasks that Madeleine just could not appreciate. The old house was simply too big for two people to manage. Half the rooms on the second floor were sealed off, and three days a week a woman came in to do the heavy work. But Tante Marie was too old to do any useful cleaning, and too stubborn not to try.

As a result, at weekends when she had no appointments, Madeleine buckled down to the double task. Back into jeans and an old shirt, she bustled upstairs and down—backbreaking work, for the most part, while her great-aunt wandered around the living-room, dining-room and parlour with a duster.

'But her heart's in the right place,' Maddie mused as she came down to get at the kitchen. 'And she does rearrange the dust very artfully!'

The kitchen was the heart of the house. Any French-Canadian could tell you that. It not only had to be clean, it had to glisten! And with Tante Marie following her around, rubbing a finger into and under and down every exposed surface it was not a task to be undertaken lightly. Which brought them to four o'clock Saturday afternoon, and shopping time.

Maddie had managed to squeeze in half an hour on the couch with her feet up. Now she struggled up, picked up the handwritten list of wants that hung on the kitchen bulletin board, made her way out to her three-year-old Omni, and took the long way around to the shopping centre. Down McGrath Street, to Church, over the bridge to Union Avenue, and north on the avenue, past Laconia High School and out to the almost empty car park of the Fairway Supermarket.

She climbed slowly out of the car. It was a hot summer day, hot as only summer sunshine can make mountain communities. Humid, too. Laconia shared its cup in the mountains with lakes in every direction, ranging from the huge body of Lake Winnipesauki, with its two hundred and eighty-three miles of shoreline, to little glacial ponds that were so small they barely owned a name. And all walled in by the rolling hills and mountain peaks that gave New Hampshire its nickname—the Granite State.

Her foot flinched as she touched it to the ground. The baked macadam covering the car park almost blistered in places. Not a bird moved in the brilliant blue sky overhead. Not a leaf swayed on drooping trees. Bag slung over her shoulder, head down, Maddie rushed for the comparative coolness of the market, only to run herself aground for the second time in her life on the broad midriff of a disgruntled male.

'Not you again!' Pulled out of her daydreams, Maddie stared up at him. Joel Fairmont, brushed and polished and shiny, dressed in casual but obviously expensive shirt and shorts—not a bit like the ragman of this morning. He looked so cool, so comfortable, that Maddie, with perspiration dripping off her forehead, was completely exasperated.

'You again?' she snapped. 'So you didn't die after all!'

'You needn't sound so disappointed,' he grumbled as he reached up to brush the lock of hair out of his eyes. 'Are you following me around?'

'Following you——!' Maddie spluttered as she ran out of appropriate English words, and shifted to French. The pithy remarks bounced off his total grin. She shifted to

German, and proceeded with a list of totally imaginary comments about his ancestry. The grin faded.

'You are a thoroughly objectionable, spoiled rotten little girl,' he snapped. 'Your aunt ought to have washed your mouth out with soap. Several times, I would imagine. Do you suppose you're the only one in these parts who can speak French and German? For your information, my mother and father *were* married—almost two years before I was born.'

Maddie drew herself up to her full height, sorry she had decided to wear flats for the shopping trip. A three-inch heel, just at that moment, would have done wonders for her ego.

'You needn't be concerned,' she rapped. 'I wouldn't follow you if you held the last two tickets on Noah's Ark!'

His grin was back. 'That bad?' he chuckled. 'Well, the more I hear the better I like. I was afraid you'd turn out to be one of those stupid women who want to fall all over me. It's good to know that my neighbour hates me!'

'I don't hate you,' Maddie replied coolly. 'That takes too much energy. I just am—indifferent to you, Mr Fairmont. Now, if you would step aside, I'd like to do my shopping. This store is bad enough without having to share it with someone like you!' She tossed her head and sniffed at him as he moved aside, allowing her room to go through the double doors and into the store itself.

'You do that very well,' laughed Joel as he followed close behind her down the fresh-vegetable aisle. 'That holier than thou bit, I mean. But what did you mean— the store is bad enough?'

Madeleine took a quick look at him over her shoulder. In the bright fluorescent lighting, some tiny portion of his midnight excesses still showed, along with a concerned look in his deep blue eyes. A look that didn't quite match up with his grin. Shopping, she thought. Most men hate shopping.

'Well, just look around you,' she snapped. 'This store was once a proud place, with all the best. Now look. Take a tomato!'

He stared down at the rack of tomatoes, stacked skilfully four and five high. 'I don't eat tomatoes,' he growled. 'My mother used to *make* me eat them. I wouldn't touch a tomato with a ten-foot pole.'

'Neither would I,' Maddie returned huffily. 'And I love tomatoes. Go ahead, pick one up.'

'They look perfect to me,' Joel argued. 'Why——'

'Pick one up,' she insisted. His hand went out slowly, fastened on the large red tomato at the top of the heap, and took it off the pile.

'Looks fine to me,' he groused.

'Yeah. Turn it over.' He did. The underside of the vegetable was bruised, and a deep soft spot had developed. Maddie tapped the spot gently with one finger.

'Five years ago they wouldn't have allowed that—thing—to even be in the store,' she snapped. 'Now they not only allow it, but they actually stack the things so a shopper in a hurry wouldn't notice the spoilage. And that, neighbour, means that not only are they selling spoiled goods, but they're doing their best to hide the fact. I detest that sort of thing! Put it down. There's no telling what you might catch from it.'

Joel's hand snapped the fruit back on to the pile as if it were fostering bubonic plague. He stood in front of the rack for a moment, rocking back and forth on the balls of his feet.

'But one tomato doesn't make a spring,' he misquoted. 'Maybe you're just trying to give the store a bad name. Why do you come here if things are so bad?'

'That's a good question,' Maddie sighed. 'But there aren't too many supermarkets in this town, you know. Now, if you'll excuse me——' She brushed by him and went over to the meat counter. As she worked her way down the aisles, she noticed that he was still in the fruit and vegetable section, turning things over one at a time. When she arrived at the check-out counter he was still working over the fruit, and a very worried store manager was standing at his elbow.

As she started to load her groceries into the back of the Omni he came out of the store, without a purchase to his name, strode over to a shiny sleek Mustang convertible parked against the store wall, and climbed in. There was anger in his every movement. Maddie finished stowing her own groceries away, then sat there in her driver's seat, bemused, as Joel made a tyre-spinning U-turn right in front of her and went racing back up Union Avenue at somewhat more than the lawful speed.

'Funny,' she muttered. 'But then he's a—funny man.' And she didn't mean 'funny—ha-ha'.

CHAPTER THREE

HENRI LEFLEUR must have been born a cherub. Some fifty years later he still retained the smooth round cheeks touched with a spot of crimson, the rotund body, perhaps a little wider at the waist than formerly, and the big smile of a jocular man. At five foot four he was not a giant, but he gave the impression of dependability, an illusion that every estate agent and used-car salesperson must possess. Only the fringe of white hair that framed his bald poll bothered him; no amount of careful combing obscured it.

'But you must recognise, Madeleine,' he insisted firmly, 'that you've done well this summer. So well that we're—er—temporarily out of houses to sell. Except——'

He left the word dangling in the breeze. Maddie recognised the trap. Nothing to sell meant no additional income. While Tante and she could *exist* on her savings and investments, there would be no icing for the cake. 'Don't forget Mrs Weathers,' she interjected. 'You know she won't do business with anyone but me. And I've been working on her for a month.'

'So all right,' he agreed, but not too enthusiastically. 'Finish up with Mrs Weathers, and then that's the end of it for a time. Except——'

Maddie looked at him carefully. No beauty, Henri LeFleur, but then again no beast. Behind that pleasant face was a minefield of brains. He was up to something. Something unpleasant, probably. So—take the plunge.

'Except what, Henri?' He got up from his chair, which squeaked in relief at being spared his considerable weight. Taking her hand in his, he led her over to the wall map and put his chubby little finger on a spot out in the Lake.

'The Murchison place?' she gasped in disbelief.

'The Murchison place,' he agreed placidly, folding his hands over the protrusion of his belly.

'But—that's been on the books for over five years,' she complained. 'You know that it's—haunted or something.'

'Ten years,' he corrected. 'And there's no such a thing as a haunted house. It's a fine estate. The whole island, thirty-five acres of good land, and a sixteen-room mansion!'

'Good land!' Maddie snorted disgustedly. 'Bare rock and moss, with as little grass as God gave Texas! Nothing but pine trees can grow well there. There are hardly four places in all those acres that are flat enough to sit down on! And it *is* haunted. That's one place that's impossible to sell. Impossible!' She walked away from the map, glowering, and deposited herself none too gently in the chair next to his desk.

'Difficult, but not impossible.' Henri followed her, sinking back into his swivel chair, a big smile lighting up his face. 'That's the test of a good salesperson, Madeleine. *Anybody* can sell the cute six-room cottage on the lakefront. It takes a *salesperson* to move the Murchison estate. It's going for a song.'

'I can't believe this,' she argued wearily. 'You're setting things up like some sort of execution. Surely there are other options?'

'Of course, my dear.' His high pleasant voice shifted into low gear, and the smile became a mournful look. 'You wouldn't have to do this sort of thing at all if you would marry me, Madeleine.'

And here we go again, Maddie sighed to herself. Henri LeFleur, the last of the swinging bachelors, and for some reason he wanted to marry Madeleine Charbonneau. It was far from the first time he had mentioned the subject, but that didn't make it any more palatable. A lovely man, Henri. He'd make somebody a fine husband. But not her! For a moment panic ran through her mind. Too much loss of income might very well drive her into the marriage trap, as it did so many women. But please God, not with Henri, she prayed.

'Henri——' She fumbled for the right words. Turn him off abruptly? Or ignore the whole thing? Her mind made up, she laid it on him. 'Henri, tell me more about the Murchison place,' she asked pleasantly.

She saw the disappointment in his eyes, but it was only a momentary thing. He reached into his desk drawer for the packet on the isolated mansion, and passed it over to her. He looked like somebody's pet dog who had just been kicked by its owner. But you'd look a lot more surprised if I accepted, Maddie wanted to scream at him. But didn't. She took the packet, weighed it in her hands, and stood up.

'I'll think it over—at home,' she promised as she turned smartly and walked out of the office.

Henri got up as he watched her tall, trim figure walk out. 'Madeleine!' he called, in protest.

'I'll think about it,' she returned solemnly over her shoulder. 'About the Murchison place, I mean.'

Her old Omni was parked in the no-parking lane just outside the old Laconia railroad station. The entire building had been converted into stores and offices after the Boston and Maine railroad had abandoned the district years before. Now, sprinkled with clean store-fronts and flower boxes, the structure smiled out on Veterans' Square and the Chamber of Commerce building.

Maddie rescued her car just seconds before a metermaid zoomed up on a motor scooter, parking tickets in hand. It was a short drive up North Main Street to Oak, and finally to McGrath and home. Tante Marie was sitting on the front porch in her rocking chair, Mehitabel asleep at her foot.

For a moment Maddie sat in the car, watching. The old lady was fast asleep, but long years of training kept the ancient body straight and starched. Only her head relaxed, lying back in one corner of the big old-fashioned rocker. She's eighty-five years old, Maddie thought apprehensively. She accepted me without question all those long years ago, and she's been both mother and father to me since. Everything I am she has made me. But she can't continue the way she's been going, and I don't seem to find the solution—how to give her what she really wants out of life.

She demands her independence, but I can't leave her alone for much longer! Something has to change around here. And for another moment panic seized her. I'm getting desperate, she told herself, barely able to restrain the feeling. But not desperate enough to take on Henri!

With a deep sigh she opened the car door carefully, closed it gently behind her, and went up the stairs. The cat stirred but kept its eyes closed. Tante Marie was breathing through her mouth, snoring. Maddie tiptoed to her side and dropped a gentle kiss on the parchment-like forehead. 'Whatever you want of me, I'll do,' she whispered. The old lady slept on as Maddie squeezed through the front door and went about her business.

Lunch over, and the series of casseroles prepared for their evening meals for the next three days, Maddie decided to take herself out on to the back porch. The task had been waiting for the past two days—any longer and the basic material would spoil. So she set up the long, folding card-table in a spot where the breeze was bound to blow, carted out all the ingredients she needed for the day, and set to it.

The two watermelons were actually leftovers from a birthday party Tante Marie had sponsored for four of the neighbourhood children. Using her sharpest paring knife, Maddie sheared off the remains of the pink fruit, then turned each piece over and carefully skinned away the hard green outside layer from the softer white rind inside. She was almost half-way through when Joel came out on to his back porch. The slam of his kitchen door caught her attention. She looked up, and caught her breath.

There was, if only for a moment, a flash of wonder in her eyes. No doubt about it, she told herself regretfully, he's a handsome man. If only handsome did as well as it looked! But the pattern had already been established. He didn't like her, and she, God save the lie, didn't like him. She recognised the lie for what it was, and blushed. 'Be honest for once in your life,' she muttered as her busy hands stilled.

He's a good man. Not perfect, by any means, but good. He stops by regularly to talk to Tante. And just because my personality has stuck crosswise in his throat there's no reason to denigrate him. Perhaps neither of us can help it, but every time we meet he aggravates me, and I aggravate him, and we both go up in flames. So what's the solution?

Solve this one problem, Maddie told herself. He lives too close to us. The only permanent solution is to get him to move away. How? Convince him that this isn't the quiet place a novelist needs. Do a little skulduggery? And then what? Where could he go? The idea hit her right in the face. Good lord, where could he go! To a place which is so isolated that even the crabs are hermits! He has money coming out of his ears. I could not only sell him the perfect house for his purposes, but I could make enough commission out of it to support Tante and me for the rest of the year! Could there be a more perfect solution? Both sides profit from it, and there's nothing but good will among us. All I have to do is sell him the Murchison mansion!

Not even recognising the big black cloud—with silver lining—that was hovering over his head, Joel was smiling, whistling, with his bird riding his shoulder. He put the protesting bird into the cage hanging from the ceiling of the veranda and came down off the porch, heading in her direction.

Maddie ducked her head quickly and went back to the paring. Anything to keep from looking into his eyes. For the first time in their acquaintance she was wearing a dress. Hidden under her apron, of course, but still a dress. Her hair was loose, and the light breeze was playing in it, stirring up the natural curls. Her work had given her rosy cheeks, and although she did not realise it, she made a beautiful figure of femininity, bent over her pan. The closer Joel came the more nervous she became. The result was inevitable. When his foot hit the bottom step, not six feet away from her, the knife slipped and drew a tiny scratch line down her index finger.

'Damn!' muttered Madeleine, lifting the injured finger to her mouth and sucking it.

'What are you doing there?' Said casually in an interested tone, as if he really cared. The idea so startled her that she snapped her head up and stared. Joel leaned against one of the roof posts, his dark-tanned face sparkling in the sun, and ran one hand through his fair hair. His only article of clothing was a pair of hiking shorts, shabbily worn, crudely patched in a couple of places. For some unaccountable reason his bare feet irritated her. He looked too comfortable; she wished she might dress the same.

'I'm busy cutting myself,' she snapped, nursing her finger.

'Here we go again,' he said wryly. 'I had hoped we could make a truce in our little war. I'm really not a bad guy, you know. Tante Marie thinks the world of me. And I like *you*. How about it?'

It had a wondrous sound to it. Pax. But it couldn't really work. If she let him through her wall of defence, then inevitably she would be a total loser. Knowing her own weaknesses, Madeleine realised that there could be no middle ground for the two of them, no place where 'like' would satisfy. It either had to be passion or hatred. And maybe the two ideas were identical. No, she thought, the only salvation for us both is separation. The plan's good; I must try it out.

'How come you're not upstairs writing?' she attacked.

'A good writer has to know when to take a break,' Joel returned softly. 'It hurts, I suppose, your hand? Do you want me to call a doctor?'

'No,' she sighed. 'Just move out of my sun. I'm trying to get a tan.'

He looked at her suspiciously. 'How far do I have to move to get out of your sun?'

'About back to your own property line,' she snapped. 'And the sooner the better!'

'What we need is a little more milk of human kindness,' Joel chuckled as he moved over beside her and ruffled her hair.

'Don't *do* that!' she said crossly as she moved away from him. 'It took me hours to comb my hair!'

'Luckily I came over to visit your aunt,' he returned, all the good humour fading away. 'So what are you making?'

'Watermelon pickles,' she muttered. All the argument had run out of her just as suddenly as it had arisen. 'It's an old family favourite.'

'I've never heard of it,' he challenged. 'An old New England recipe?'

'Not exactly,' she laughed. 'An old Tennessee recipe. Try one if you dare.' She pointed to the sealed bottle on the table next to her work materials. 'That's the last bottle from last year.'

Joel struggled with the opening, then used her knife to spear one of the little brown fingerlets. 'Hey,' he said enthusiastically, 'that's good!' He wiped off her knife and handed it back to her, and she could see the frown forming on his face.

'If you can make fancies like this, how come your aunt has to do all the cooking in the house? She's no spring chicken, you know.'

Maddie rose slowly to her feet, trying to contain herself. Her uncle the police chief would look very poorly at the idea of her stabbing this monster to death with a paring knife. And as she hesitated, she thought. Of course it made sense. Tante Marie *did* prepare all the meals. She took out the casseroles and pre-frozen dinners that Maddie constructed in between jobs, and she put them in the oven to warm. *Voilà*. And all she had to do was to explain all this to Mr Nosey, right? At which point her temper intervened.

Why should I explain anything to this—ogre? Maddie thought. First, it's none of his business; second I don't care what he thinks, do I? So why explain?

'I don't see that it's any of your business what the internal arrangements of my house are,' she said in a very frosty tone. 'If you have some pressing business elsewhere, you won't let me keep you, will you?'

'Oh no, not at all,' returned Joel. 'I have a date with your aunt. Every day at this time we get together. There's a lot we have to talk about, your aunt and I. Funny, this is the first time that——'

'Don't drink that stuff!' she yelled at him as he sampled a bucket of what looked to be water. He snatched his finger back as if burnt.

'What is it?' he asked, wiping his finger off on his chest.

'Lime water,' she told him stiffly. 'After I cut the rind up into little fingerlets I rinse it all off in clear water and then I soak it for twenty-four hours in lime water. Now, if you wouldn't mind, perhaps you could take yourself off. I think Tante is still napping, and I wouldn't want her disturbed.'

'Gawd!' he sighed. 'You may not be totally imposs- ible, but you're working hard to get there, aren't you? Your only trouble, girl, is that you're basically nice, so all this bad temper is just wasted! I really don't know why I like you.'

'So go,' she snarled at him. 'It'll make us both happy.'

Joel gave her another long searching look, then turned around and marched down the stairs. As his foot hit the ground he looked back over his shoulder. 'What we need,' he announced, 'is a fence. Or maybe a wall!' He walked off, and left an ineffable hole in Maddie's life. No sooner had he gone into his own house than Tante Marie bustled out on to the porch.

'Has Mr Fairmont come?' the old lady asked anxiously. 'I was doing my hair, and——'

'Come and gone,' Maddie said firmly. 'What a de- testable man he is, Tante!'

'Is he really?' her aunt asked with a puzzled look. 'You know, I find him very sweet. He comes every day, you know. We talk. He's teaching me to play fan-tan.'

'So he says,' Maddie sighed. 'That's a Chinese gam- bling game, isn't it? Look, I'm sorry, Tante Marie, if I broke up a beautiful friendship, but—well, I guess I lost my temper again. Do you want me to call him back?'

'No, no,' said Tante Marie, doing her best to be solemn in the face of her great-niece's obvious discomfort. 'Not at all. I can catch up with him tomorrow. Maybe we could invite him for supper?'

'I'd rather not,' Maddie snapped. 'There's just so much—oh, Tante, I don't know why I let my temper run away with me. I really don't. This is *your* home. If you want to invite Mr Fairmont to supper, by all means let's do it.'

She bent to her task again, her fingers busy, and her mind on something else. In the distance she could hear the shrill piercing sound of the penny whistle, played by someone who obviously didn't know what he was doing. It continued, wavering louder and softer, for most of the afternoon, and certainly could not have added a single line to his novel!

Her aunt came to the door twice to look. Her favourite child, Madeleine Charbonneau, and the old lady's heart twisted just a little at the thought of that child growing old as a spinster. She looked up, over Maddie's shining brown curls. Joel Fairmont was sitting on his porch rail, a can of beer in his hand, teasing his parrot. Tante Marie shook her head and wished for a miracle.

Time often takes things in hand when least wanted. Maddie woke up the next morning with the insecure feeling that she had no work to go to, and the concurrent headache that came from listening to sourly played whistles well into the night. But a few telephone calls in the neighbourhood last night had set the stage, and here was the first act of the play.

Outside her window two clumps of little boys were gathered, hovering over an innocent soccer ball. At the blast of a whistle they had at it. Eighteen little boys, eighteen big voices, all yelling at fever pitch as they attacked the ball, the grass, each other, and Tante Marie's favourite petunias.

Maddie grinned at herself, hustled through her shower and into her blue jeans and painting blouse. This was no time to dilly-dally. She raced downstairs, snatching her official whistle from the hook behind the door, and went out to referee the fray.

The game began at eight o'clock. At nine Joel Fairmont came out on his back porch to watch. At nine-thirty, when both teams were stretched out, exhausted, all over the grass, he came marching down towards her, death and destruction written plain on his brow.

'How,' he grated, 'am I supposed to do any writing with all this noise?'

'Why, I don't understand,' Maddie simpered. 'The boys have to practise. They can't use the park today, so, as usual, I let them use my yard.'

'Our yard,' Joel corrected glumly. 'You mean this goes on all the time?'

'Oh no,' she exclaimed. 'Only during the vacation. During the school year there's the tennis team, the football team, the girls' hockey team and the track team. It gets pretty noisy by then, of course. This is a relatively quiet time.' She put her whistle to her lips and blew a mighty blast. 'Come on, boys,' she called, 'time for the second period!'

'Just a damn minute,' shouted Joel over the din. 'I'm not going to put up with this! At least you can get them off *my* part of the lawn!'

'Wouldn't be big enough,' she shouted back. 'Need the whole area. You can't fence these kids in, you know!'

'I don't know any such damn thing!' he growled at her, and stamped off towards his own house.

Maddie saw neither hide nor hair of him for the rest of the day. The soccer game broke for lunch, and was succeeded by a hockey game all afternoon, and Madeleine went to bed with a very large grin on her face.

The next morning she woke to a considerably different noise. Outside, a truck had pulled up between the two houses, and a trio of men were working at something loudly enough to awaken the wooden Indian in the park.

She slid out of bed and pattered barefoot over to the back windows. The truck was from Cutler Builders, or so the sign on its yellow back boasted. The men were unloading material from the bed of the truck, and spacing it out on the ground, stretching a line from McGrath Street to the boundary of the park.

'Where is that man?' muttered Maddie as she raced through the kitchen, still pulling on her sweat-shirt.

'Joel?' Her aunt was busy at the back window, watching. 'Out on the running track, I think. A nice man.'

'I'll nice him,' Maddie grumbled. 'I'll nice him up into a million pieces and feed him to his parrot!'

'Madeleine!' Tante Marie's wail followed her out of the door as she spurted towards the park and the running track, doing her best not to look at the workmen—who stopped what they were doing and looked at her with a great deal of interest and a couple of sharp whistles. It's hard to sniff disdainfully when one is running; she almost tripped over the board surface that outlined the cinder track.

She was sitting on the bench just beyond the Indian statue when Joel came puffing around the corner of the track. He pulled up beside her, and dropped, wiping his head with the towel from around his neck.

'So—you hide yourself here every morning?' Maddie looked up, shading her eyes against the sun. Joel, looking disgustingly healthy, clothed in a disreputable set of running togs, smiled down at her. She clamped her mind shut against the terrible yearning, and all of a sudden she didn't want to talk to him about anything.

'I'll close my eyes,' she muttered, 'and count to ten, after which you will have disappeared back into wherever you came from, right?' Her hair had come loose, and she was unable to find the little blue ribbon. Using both hands on either side of her head, she ran her fingers through the mess and wished mightily she had kept it in braids.

'Don't do that,' he protested mildly. 'I like it all loose and fluffy.'

'Well, I don't,' she snapped. 'Don't you have some pressing business? A few sentences to parse—something like that?'

'Like Old Faithful,' he chuckled, 'I can always depend on my welcome. Did you notice that I took your suggestion?'

'That can't be,' she sighed. 'You're still here!'

'Not that one!' He put one foot up on the bench, too close to her for comfort, and leaned on the knee. 'The other one—about the fence?'

'Fence?' she echoed. 'It was entirely your idea. I've lived in that house for twenty-seven years, and we *never* needed a fence until *you* came along!' She edged carefully away from his foot. A thing of major importance, that. Madeleine Charbonneau required her own living space, and any encroachment on it made her extremely nervous. It got worse when Joel took his foot away, then sat down next to her. She gave a little squeak and moved to the end of the bench.

'I don't bite, you know,' Joel growled. She had ducked her head a moment earlier. Now she looked up just in time to catch the frown on his face.

'I wasn't to know that,' she growled back at him. 'Your parrot does, why shouldn't you? Where *is* Bluebeard, by the way?'

'Over at your house,' he chuckled. 'Tante Marie——'

'She's *my* aunt, not yours,' Maddie protested. 'Her name is Mrs Tetrault!'

'She told me to call her Tante Marie,' he assured her in a soft pleasant voice. 'Anyway, your aunt offered to take care of the little devil while I'm away in Boston.'

There it is again, Maddie told herself. That crazy feeling, just because he's announced that he has to be away. Why does it make me feel so rotten? 'How long?' she asked, and the misery she felt was reflected in her voice.

That look was back on his face again. Concern, charm, and something else that Maddie just could not lay a handle to.

'Two or three days,' he told her, and there was something of sorrow in his voice too. 'Maybe longer. My mother has a problem. Good lord, my mother *always* has a problem. Mainly with me, I'm sorry to say. I am, perhaps, not the finest son in the world. No comment? No smart remarks?'

'My sympathy is all with your mother,' Maddie told him. 'The poor put-upon woman is probably suffering from nerves!' She clapped her hands over her mouth. That was not at all what she had meant to say. This morning was a time to be wily, to be cunning, to get Joel thinking, 'Move away from McGrath Street.' And

instead she had flared up instantly in defence of a woman
she had never met. Joel's eyes lit up with an unholy glee.
He did that on purpose, she told herself grimly. He loves
to see me shoot off like a Roman candle! The man is a
positive threat to my peace of mind! 'Go away,' she
muttered desperately. 'Please!'

'Well,' said Joel contemplatively, 'it's about time.
Most of them fall in love with me in four hours. You're
taking too much time, Madeleine Charbonneau!'

'Why, you conceited arrogant arrant ass!' she shouted
as she jumped to her feet. 'You've got about as much
manners and common sense as a—a wooden Indian!'
She whirled around so he could not see the tears, and
started racing up the cinder path, away from Joel. His
raucous laugh followed her all the way past the statue.
And there was no doubt about it. The wooden Indian
winked at her as she went by.

Tante Marie was sitting at the kitchen table when Maddie
came in. The old lady was stirring her cup of tea, and
saying, 'Oh my!' to anyone who would listen. The audience included Bluebeard, perched on top of the refrigerator, and Mehitabel, patrolling the small open space
on the floor between the table and the sink. Maddie took
one look at the mess on the floor, and opened the back
screen door.

'Mehitabel. Out!' she commanded, and for once the
cat obeyed.

She closed the door behind the big white cat and
hurried over to her aunt to comfort. 'What happened,
Tante?'

'Well, I'm not quite sure,' muttered her aunt, confused. 'Joel asked me last night to take care of his bird

for a time, and he came down this morning, asking for you. And then Mehitabel came in—and the bird—I don't remember. Somehow one of them knocked the mixing bowl out of my hand. That's your pancake breakfast all over the floor——'

'Don't bother about the mess,' soothed Maddie. 'I'll get to it in a minute. Then what happened?'

'Then the bird—I never knew birds could—what language!'

Bluebeard had stopped to listen to the conversation, and when the cat disappeared out of the door he began to strut. 'Crazy cat,' he squawked. 'Awk! Lookit the lovely knockers!'

Maddie stalked over to the broom closet, and came out armed. 'One more smart remark out of you,' she said firmly, 'and you're soup stock!' She waved the broom in the bird's face. It was a convincing threat. Bluebeard jumped heavily into flight, and zoomed up to the top of the curtain rod, where he cocked his head and glared at them for a moment. 'Hard-hearted Hannah,' he squawked, then tucked his head under his wing and went to sleep.

'It's nothing to worry about, Tante,' Maddie comforted. 'I'll get this place cleaned up, and then I'll go over and get the bird's cage. I don't have to go to work for a couple of days, so it'll be no real trouble. Why don't you go out on the front porch and get some rest? Your club is coming this afternoon, isn't it?'

The old lady's face brightened immeasurably. 'Yes,' she said. 'This afternoon! And the parrot will be here. Do you suppose you could make him talk while the ladies are here?' She looked up anxiously at her great-niece.

She had learned over a number of years that Madeleine could do anything, if asked correctly.

'I'm sure the bird will talk,' Maddie assured her. 'But I can't guarantee that you'll like what he'll say. Are you sure you want me to bring him in?'

There was no need for Tante Marie to answer. It was all there in her expression; awe, delight, like a little child with the first ice-cream cone of the year.

Tante was so affected that Maddie offered her an arm as she walked out to the front porch and relaxed in her favourite chair. The footstool arranged, and a very light blanket thrown over her to ward off the occasionally cool winds off the bay, and in a moment she was fast asleep, her dreams running in cheerful laughter over her wrinkled face.

Maddie sat for a few more minutes, watching her dearest relative sleep, remembering. Tante Marie had closed up her own little house in Lakeport and moved into the house on McGrath Street twenty-five years ago when two-year-old Maddie was suddenly orphaned. And she had soothed all the knee scrapes, all the tears, all the heartaches away. Which I shall never forget, Maddie told herself firmly. She patted the sleeping figure on top of her head, and made for the kitchen.

The clean-up was a little more than she had anticipated. Pancake dough, left to dry, is a hard subject to remove. It was splattered all over the floor, and on two walls. When that task was done, it was time to do something about the watermelon pickles.

The kitchen smelled of a dozen teasing scents when she had finished. She detoured by the front porch. Tante was still fast asleep. Maddie adjusted her blankets, then made her way upstairs to the bathroom. It was a quiet

day. The men and their truck had gone, and in their
place was a five-foot chain-link fence, stretching from
McGrath Street to Opechee Park. Less than a dozen
children were playing in the park, and with the school
vacation in full spate, hardly a car approached the north
end of McGrath. She filled the tub as far as the hot
water heater would allow, and wallowed in sybaritic
luxury.

She had left the bathroom door open, as usual, in
case Tante called for help. But it wasn't Tante who disturbed her dreams, it was Bluebeard. The old parrot,
beating the air desperately, flew up the stairwell and into
the bathroom, where he perched on the edge of the tub,
cocked his head to one side, and stared at her.

'Awk. Pretty baby,' the bird squawked. 'Polly want
a cracker? Lookit the lovely knockers!'

'Now that's enough of that!' Maddie sat up, trying to
hide her impressive upper structure, when the stupidity
of it all struck her, and she broke out in giggles. As-
suming that birds had real intelligence! Hah! And just
because he's a male bird, being embarrassed by it all!
Double hah! And then, thinking somehow that the parrot
would go home to Joel and give him a full report! And
me a college graduate, for heaven's sake!

Nevertheless she chased the bird from his perch and
climbed out of the tub, carefully shielding herself from
that uncanny eye, and avoiding the wall mirror. There
was nothing she wanted to see in that! Fairy godmothers
and magic mirrors were few and far between in the
mountains of New Hampshire!

Which brought her downstairs just in time to check
the simmering pickles, set up Tante Marie's card-tables,
and welcome the five elderly members of the bridge club.

They had been coming to the house once a week for twenty-two years, and without fail Mrs Mahoney would say, 'My, how you've grown, Madeleine!'

Tante Marie was already awake, bright-eyed and bushy-tailed. Mrs Mahoney was the last arrival, bustling in like a fresh breeze. 'My, how you've grown, Madeleine!' she said. Maddie dimpled, escorted them all to the parlour, and went back to the kitchen, wondering if the ladies knew that nobody ever used the parlour, except for this weekly group.

The parlour was set aside. One used it for funerals, for visits from the parish priest, and, if a girl was lucky, for that one moment when that one man made conversation about weddings and children and things of that nature. It hadn't had much use lately.

Madeleine stirred the simmering pickles, then remembering her promise, hurried up to Joel's house for Bluebeard's cage, which was hanging on the back porch. And ran into her first obstacle. For some reason she had assumed he would have a gate installed in the fence. Not so. She gritted her teeth and vaulted over.

Cage in hand, she stalked back home, managed with some difficulty to corner Bluebeard and stuffed him inside his travelling cell. 'Hey, pretty baby,' the bird chanted mournfully as he hopped up on to his swinging trapeze.

'Well, you brought it on yourself,' Maddie told him firmly. The bird stood on the trapeze bar glaring at her, then suddenly shut his eyes and seemed to collapse, hanging from the bar with a grip of iron, but upside down.

'Oh, damn!' snorted Maddie as she hurried to open the cage and peer inside. 'Bluebeard! Damn, if I've killed his bird he'll do the same to me. Bluebeard!'

The bird opened one eye and stared at her. 'Awk,' he squawked. 'Fooled you, baby!' Maddie slammed the cage door shut in disgust, and carried bird and cage into the parlour for the edification of the bridge club.

So by the time the ladies had gone, Tante had been fed her supper, the bottles had been sterilised and the pickles bottled and put away in the cool cellar for the required six weeks, Maddie was exhausted. Nevertheless she went out on to the back porch and stared at that fence. If only I were a witch, she thought vehemently. I'd put such a curse on Joel Fairmont he wouldn't be able to sit down for a month! Or even worse, I'll marry the man! That ought to teach him something!

Yes, the voice of her conscience agreed sarcastically. That ought to teach somebody something.

But it had been a long, hard day, and she was tired. She made a hex-gesture towards the fence, and her shoulders drooped. The kitchen door slammed, and Tante Marie came to stand behind her.

'What have you been up to, Madeleine?' her aunt asked gently.

'Just finishing off the watermelon pickles,' she returned.

'That's nice,' commented Tante Marie, and went back inside to check up on her knitting needles.

CHAPTER FOUR

'I DON'T know when I've been so tired,' Madeleine told Tante Marie as she collapsed into a chair. 'That fool woman walked me through three different houses in one day!'

'But you sold her the last one?' Her aunt was making tea in the old Breton manner, and turned around to pat her great-niece on the shoulder.

'But I sold her the last one,' Maddie repeated, with a very self-satisfied smirk. 'And I'm afraid it *is* the last one. I had to cry on Henri's shoulder to get him to let me handle the sale. Usually a salesperson makes eight or nine sales a year. I've made ten so far this year, and Henri says I have to come to a halt and give the other salesmen a break!'

'Unfair, to cry on Henri,' her aunt commented. 'It takes skill, charm and tact to sell things. You have them all. I don't know why, with all that Charbonneau blood in you!'

'Oh, Tante,' Madeleine chuckled, 'that was so long ago. Are you never going to forgive your sister for marrying my grandfather?' She took a satisfying sip of the strong brew. 'Speaking of blood, what have you heard from Attila the Hun? I haven't seen him for a week.'

'Attila the—oh, you mean Mr Fairmont. Joel?' The old lady's face cracked into a big smile, then instantly sobered. 'I'm afraid Joel is unhappy with our neighbourhood.'

'How so?' asked Maddie. She shifted in her chair to relieve the pressure on one tired leg, and finger-brushed her lush brown hair back off her face. 'What have we done now?'

'I don't know,' Tante mused. 'At first it was the kids playing in the yard, and then there were all those nasty signs, and a couple of days ago one of those field hockey teams were out in the street in front of his house and wouldn't go away. Every day it's been something, and all very disturbing. I told him you had friends in all those athletic groups, because of your own sports record, and I suggested he get you to take a hand. Funny, that. He walked off mumbling something about how he was going to get a hand on you—lord, he was angry! And now yesterday afternoon——'

'What, yesterday afternoon?' Maddie prodded.

Tante Marie wrung her hands, distressed. 'He said Mehitabel was hunting his parrot. What a silly idea *that* is! As if my cat would want to eat a tough old bird like that! Forty years old, Joel said.'

Maddie almost choked on her tea, and was crying by the time the spasms had passed. 'You mean to tell me that *Joel* is forty——'

'Don't be silly,' snorted Tante Marie. 'The parrot. Joel is only thirty-three. Bluebeard? Is that what they call the bird?'

'Yeah, Bluebeard. That's pretty old, even for a parrot.'

'They live a long time,' her aunt mused. 'Just think, I'm twice as old as the bird!' It was a some sort of private joke. The old lady almost doubled up in laughter, while her great-niece stared in stupefaction as dry cackles filled the kitchen.

'So where is the great white hunter?'

'Why, he hasn't come home,' her aunt reported. 'Not since this morning. I haven't any idea——'

The kitchen windows were open to trap any movement of air, and suddenly air was moving in very large quantities, to the cacophony of sound bounding down from the house next door. A mixture of wild shouts, parrot curses, and cat yowls, loud enough to awaken the Indian statue.

'Dear God, he's killing our cat!' Maddie shouted as she scrabbled for her shoes.

'Surely not,' Tante Marie said plaintively. 'Such a nice man!'

'You can hear him at it!' Maddie insisted as she headed for the back door and went charging across the open grass between the two houses, shouting some incomprehensible war cry of her own as she vaulted over his new fence.

Joel Fairmont came out of his own back door as Madeleine thundered up the stairs.

'What the hell!' he complained. 'Isn't it enough that your damn cat assaults me, without *you* joining in?'

Maddie skidded to a stop, losing one of her shoes in the effort, and stared at him. He was shirtless, and along the shoulder where skin met undershirt, four parallel lines oozed blood.

'What——' she stammered.

'Your damn cat scratched the hell out of me!' he roared, clamping his arm with his other hand. 'Isn't the blood enough, or do I have to get a signed confession?'

'My cat would *never* attack a human being,' she said very firmly. 'He has a deep and abiding love for humans. So what did you do to *force* him to defend himself?'

Joel gave her a sarcastic look. 'Look, little girl, your damn cat sneaked into my house when my back was turned, attacked my parrot with intent to kill, jumped on me when I tried to protect my bird—dear God, where has Bluebeard gone?'

'Who cares?' she snapped back at him. 'Where's my cat!'

'To hell with your cat!' he roared. The blast of his anger almost knocked Maddie back off the porch. She put out a hand to the rail, and hung on. 'My bird is a geriatric case,' Joel continued. 'Bluebeard can't stand this sort of excitement! One of these minutes he could drop dead from a heart attack!'

'It couldn't happen to a nicer bird,' she agreed. 'And I suppose you mean to tell me that your bird did nothing to aggravate the situation? No loud-mouthing, no taunts, no putting up a fence to needle your neighbours?'

'No!' he snapped at her. 'Can't you get it through your head? Your cat attacked my bird and me. Now where—Bluebeard!' he shouted at the top of his lungs. Up from the roof-tree there came a little flutter, as a very frightened parrot squawked, 'Pretty baby, pretty baby, pretty baby.' After which Bluebeard took to the air, soared heavily around in a descending circle, and made a perfect four-point landing on Maddie's shoulder. And no amount of coaxing could get him to transfer to Joel.

'Now see what you've done,' Joel muttered as he offered a finger to Bluebeard for transportation. The bird ducked its head and began pruning its feathers, as if Joel

Fairmont's shoulder were the last thing in the world he wanted.

'Who, me? Look what *I've* done! Your bird's finally wising up!' Madeleine summoned up her best 'drop-dead' look and threw it at him, to no avail.

'Yes, look what you've done. You're not satisfied with setting your cat on me, you've also got to alienate my parrot! I'd think you'd be ashamed of yourself!'

'I'd bet you would think that,' she agreed, spitting fire. 'Now where is my cat!'

He waved a hand towards the door. 'This house has fourteen rooms and twenty-two cupboards,' he announced. 'Your cat is somewhere in that maze, unless he went out of the window the way Bluebeard did!'

'My cat doesn't fly,' snapped Maddie. 'I think I'll take you to court for maintaining an attractive nuisance. Now, are you going to bring me my cat?'

'Not on your life,' Joel said gloomily. Little droplets of blood were still running down his arm. Maddie suddenly realised, with remorse, that he really had a nasty scratch.

'I could bandage your shoulder,' she offered contritely. He drew away as if she should be ringing a leprosy bell and crying 'unclean!'

'Not on your life,' Joel groaned. 'I'd rather have Bluebeard do my nursing than you. Everything you touch, lady, turns to—well—go find your damn cat!'

'He's not a *damn* cat,' she muttered angrily under her breath as she went through the kitchen, heading for the main rooms downstairs. Dishes were piled up mile-high in the sink. The place smelled of something hidden and rancid; ignoring it all, she stalked through the swinging doors, calling Mehitabel at every step.

The living-room looked no better. Someone had made a casual effort to pick up the overturned furniture left from the party, but beyond that, 'clean' looked to be only a word in the dictionary. Maddie went through every room on that floor, to no avail. Her cat was not numbered among the piles of junk. Halfway up the stairs Bluebeard abandoned her.

'What's up, baby?' the parrot squawked. Maddie came to a halt. It was hard to believe that the bird had only a random vocabulary and practically no comprehension.

'I'm looking for my cat,' she said firmly.

The word was enough. 'Cat!' the bird squalled, launching himself clumsily into the air. Flying was not Bluebeard's strong suit. Maybe age had something to do with it. The bird circled her head a couple of times, then came to rest on the chandelier and watched her with those beady eyes, head cocked to one side. Like his owner, Maddie reminded herself, as she tried to build up a head of indignation again.

There was a somnolent silence on the second floor, and the door to the attic was closed, which meant a room-by-room search was required. With no obvious choice available, she started at the far right-hand side and worked her way down the corridor. Only the last room on the left seemed inhabited. A small bed was pushed up against the wall, unmade of late. A typewriter stand and a deep comfortable office chair were placed directly in front of the open window, the only exit point on the floor. So if the bird escaped from here, she thought, where's Mehitabel? She called the name cautiously.

A cautious wail from the old cat, from outside the window! Madeleine stifled a little scream and ran, pushing the typewriter on its portable stand completely out of the way. A stack of papers, balanced precariously on the side-tray of the typewriter stand, quivered and collapsed on to the floor.

Paying no attention to the commotion she was creating, Maddie leaned out of the window, her heart in her mouth. Just outside, inches beyond her reach, was a small ornamental gable, and Mehitabel roosted on its inclined roof, clinging for dear life.

'Oh, my——!' muttered Madeleine. She leaned out as far as safety would allow, and stretched out a hand. The cat mewed, but did not stir to help, and Madeleine had no more inches to offer.

'What the hell are you doing now!' Joel came into the room behind her and strode over to the window. 'Why, you certifiable little idiot!' he snapped as he took a firm grip on the back of her trousers.

'My cat!' she screamed back at him. 'He can't see all that well. Your damn bird tricked him into this!'

'He wouldn't have gone after the bird if you'd feed him more often,' he argued from behind her. 'Come on, girl. You don't fly either, and it's a long way down from here!'

Maddie took a look around her, and almost swallowed her tongue. It *was* a long way down, and she was not all that comfortable with heights. 'Pull me in,' she begged.

Joel obliged with a massive heave. The back seam on her trousers gave, she came hurtling back into the room to smash into his typewriter stand, and both she and the machine crashed to the ground.

'What—what are you doing!' she screamed at him as she tried to struggle back to her feet. Her eye caught his typewriter. There was an ominous slant to its paper roll, but she had troubles of her own. Her trousers had split all the way down the seam, and it required both her hands to keep herself covered. She ached in several places, which only added to her anger.

'Why, you—you monster!' she screamed at him. 'Look what you've done!'

'I am looking,' Joel sighed. 'God, how did anyone let you live long enough to be twenty-five?'

'Twenty-seven,' she interjected fiercely. 'Look at my trousers! I only bought them two weeks ago!'

'You shouldn't patronise Good Will Industries for your clothes,' he growled. 'Look at my typewriter. I only bought it three weeks ago! And my manuscript!' His voice went up almost half an octave as he dropped to his knees and scrambled to gather up the scattered papers.

'Hah!' snorted Maddie, struggling to keep her derriere covered. 'Only a bunch of papers! The way you keep this house no one would know the difference between manuscripts and waste paper. Slopsville!'

'If I have lost any pages of this manuscript,' he said slowly and grimly, enunciating each little syllable separately, 'I am going to break every bone in your body, starting with your left little finger and working my way around to your right little toe! Do you understand that, woman!'

It wasn't the threat that bothered Madeleine. It was the entire sequence of the day. She dropped to her knees beside him, and began gathering up papers with both hands. Unconsciously she scanned each page. A romance novel! So that's what he does, she told herself vaguely.

'Get your hands off those papers!' wailed Joel, snatching at the collection she had gathered. The top two pages tore almost exactly down the middle. He came slowly to his feet, glaring sudden death at her. Maddie came up as well, in the gracefully smooth movement of an athlete. One hand was at her mouth, to hold back the dry hacking sobs that were shaking her.

'Don't you dare hit me,' she managed to squeeze out. It was almost like a password. His brow furrowed, then cleared. The anger faded, to be replaced by a tiny little smile.

'No,' he said, and the smile grew to a grin of mammoth proportions, 'I never hit girls.' Maddie backed away from the derisive smile, until her back was to the wall. A different kind of fear crammed into her mind, dispersing everything else. A fear and an excitement. Her anger was gone faster than it had risen, but her arms were trembling as she brought them up in front of her.

'So you don't like fences,' he mused. 'It's not true about fences and good neighbours?'

'I'd rather you hit me,' Maddie said hoarsely, dropping into the 'guard' position.

'I don't give choices,' he returned heartily. 'Come on now, take it like a man—I mean, a woman!'

There was a soft plop at the window. Out of the corner of her eye Maddie noted that Mehitabel had effected his own rescue. Her mind relieved, she turned back to Joel, totally ready to pulverise him—arms ready, hands cocked, feet prepared to kick, but mind empty. So when he walked up to her and wrapped her up in his arms, she was already in a state of dazed anticipation.

'Don't do that,' she said, her voice thick with suppressed emotions.

'You mean this?' Joel's face hovered over hers as she shut her eyes. His lips touched, light as a butterfly, then returned again for another sip. Soft, sweet exploration forced the barrier of her clenched lips as if it were no defence at all. His hand swept around her, to the curve of her hips, pulling her hard up against him, melding them for a precious moment into two parts of the same being. No flames—just a roiling in the pit of her stomach, and a warmth as blood flowed faster. And a rushing noise in her ears that blotted out all the other sounds. The soft whisper of the breeze at the window disappeared, as did the shouts from the kids at the baseball field. Nothing remained except him. And you hate it, her conscience noted sardonically. She waved one free hand vaguely, as if to bat away such a crazy thought, and purely by accident hit him right in the eye as he broke off the kiss.

'Good God,' he muttered as he staggered back from her. 'In addition to everything else, you've almost put my eye out!'

It was just enough to set off the tinder again. 'You deserve it,' she shouted at him at the top of her voice. 'You deserve everything that happens to you, you—you monster! I hope you get gangrene—or whatever!'

'What?' he grated, and if looks could kill, there would have been a double murder right in that room.

'I——' she stuttered, then swept up her cat under her arm and ran for the stairs as if the devil pursued her. It wasn't until she was out on the porch, and the screen door slammed behind her, that she realised that the devil was *not* pursuing her, and neither was Joel

Fairmont. And the thought startled her because of the heart-pain it produced.

'A fine figure of a man,' Tante Marie mused as she came back from the window a few days later. 'He's been over to the park to play ball with the kids.'

'They'd better look out. He'll steal the fillings out of their teeth and their baseball as well,' Madeleine muttered. She was coiled up on the sofa in the living-room, her feet tucked up under her. It was still early—no more than seven o'clock, with an hour and a half of daylight left, but Madeleine had come home exhausted after a long day looking for sideline jobs. A long, hot bath had done a little to soothe her spirits, and now she was relaxed, decked out in an old pair of ragged shorts and a worn T-shirt, ready for a late supper.

'I'm for an early bed tonight,' she announced. 'And a long, slow weekend. I think I'll go down to the Weir on Monday. Henri said I could borrow his runabout for the day. Would you like to take a trip, Tante?'

'Me? In one of those crazy speedboats? Not on your life!'

Maddie shrugged her shoulders. At her age Tante Marie chose her own sports and her own times. 'Oh, well,' she commented, 'I can go by myself.'

'Not safe,' her aunt insisted. 'Not safe at all. Well, will you look at that!'

'Will I look at what?'

'Why, Mr Fairmont is coming in our direction. He just jumped right over the fence. My, how athletic! And he's coming our way. Isn't that nice?'

Maddie bounced off the sofa as if she had been stabbed. 'Coming here?' she gasped. 'Not—no, it *isn't* nice! Lock the doors! Turn out the lights and we'll make believe we're not home!'

'What kind of silliness is that?' Tante Marie exclaimed. 'Where are your manners, Madeleine! The poor man probably wants someone to talk to. Some adult!' The old lady primped up her hair and dress, and started for the back door, smiling.

'Don't let him in!' Maddie screeched. 'He probably wants to finish what he started last week!' But her warning was too late. She could hear her aunt's pleasant treble welcome the ogre, and invite him in. And here I stand in my fanciest clothes, she thought. Why am I always at a disadvantage when that—man—is around?

There was an exchange of conversation in the kitchen, but too short to allow her to dash for the stairs. Nervously she re-tied the shoelace that held her hair in a ponytail, then sank back into the softness of the couch and picked up a magazine. Stonewall it. If the President can do it, so can I! Lady Madeleine Charbonneau, at home, modelling the finest evening wear of the season! Unfortunately for her mission, the magazine she had selected at random was the *Sporting News*.

'Will you look who's here!' Tante Marie warbled as she came into the living-room, ushering Joel in front of her. The old lady looked excited, as if she had reached one objective on her path towards greater goals.

Maddie lowered her magazine and looked him up and down coolly. Even her great-aunt could feel the temperature drop. 'Oh, who?' asked Maddie.

'Why, Mr Fairmont, of course!' Tante Marie fluttered around the room like a humming bird, putting unneeded housekeeping touches to the bric-à-brac that filled the shelves.

'Oh, him,' Maddie muttered under her breath.

'Madeleine!' her aunt snapped, and all the automatic functions that had been drilled into Madeleine since she was a two-year-old snapped into action.

Almost without her own volition she heard someone with *her* voice say, 'Good evening, Mr Fairmont. To what do we owe this honour?'

'And I'll just go and get it ready,' Tante Marie avowed. She was gone before Madeleine could discover what *it* was, sweeping out of the room as only a Gibson Girl could.

Opposite the sofa, Joel prodded one of the chairs as if he thought it might bite, then settled into it. For a man who had just been playing baseball with children, he looked remarkably neat, Maddie noted. Not a hair out of place, not a sign of perspiration—and not an inch of smile.

'I like your aunt,' he announced ponderously, like a diplomat declaring a state of war. He had both hands on his knees, eyes spearing Maddie like bayonets.

'So do I,' she snapped. 'My great-aunt, actually.' She stared back at him, then moved restlessly to get her feet flat on the floor, knees together, back straight. She had to tug at the legs of her shorts to get them down. The whole idea of him staring at her legs added to her nervousness. Her legs, she had decided years ago, were too long for the rest of her.

'I wouldn't want your aunt mixed up in this game you and I are playing,' Joel said quietly. It might have been the first time she had ever heard him speak in so low a voice. His baritone had resonance and timbre to it, totally attractive—in some less arrogant and arrant man she added to herself.

'I'm not playing any games,' she answered stiffly. The temperature in the room went down another ten degrees. No way am I going to surrender to this—person, she lectured herself fiercely. *No way!* 'Perhaps you'd care to tell me what brings you here?'

'I had a long alk with my mother,' he began, 'and she——'

'I'm glad you had a chance to see your mother,' Maddie interrupted sweetly. 'Now, to what do we owe this pleasure?'

'Why, your aunt invited me to have a late snack,' he said, witl a little chuckle. 'She noticed that I hadn't eaten.'

'Oh, she just looked in your eye and saw that, did she?' Maddie asked sarcastically. 'Your house is off limits, but mine isn't? Isn't that what your fence says?'

'Why, I thought it was your aunt's house,' he countered, ignoring entirely the part about the fence. 'Does it upset your digestion to eat with a gentleman?'

I don't know,' she snapped, 'and I won't find out tonight, unless one happens to show up unexpectedly. And this is *my* house.'

'Then perhaps I'd better go.' Joel started to get up before Maddie realised what a terrible thing she had said.

'No—please,' she begged. 'Don't go. That was a terrible thing for me to say. I *do* own the house, but it's Tante Marie's *home*, and if she wants to invite the devil himself to dinner, then she's perfectly correct to do so.'

Joel sank back into the chair, grinning. 'And she did, didn't she?' he queried. 'Invite the devil, I mean!'

'I was just using an old cliché,' she answered bitterly, then tried her best to change the subject. 'I hope your bird is better?'

'Better than what?' he challenged. 'Parrots can live for a long time, but Bluebeard is pushing right along. I don't think he measures days as better or worse, not any more '

'I wasn't trying to insinuate anything,' she complained. 'I was just—would you rather talk about the weather? Or your fence?'

'Not particularly. Somehow I get the idea that the fence was a mistake. But my mother wanted it, and it's her house, you know. What else is there to talk about in this town?'

Maddie stared at him, shocked by what he had said. His *mother's* house. *She* wanted a fence! And all the time Madeleine Charbonneau had been blaming him, building an upside-down pyramid on the tiniest bit of misinformation in the world!

'Oh, lots of things,' she gabbled to hide her confusion. 'Life and death and babies, and all the things the tourists bring in. And it's your mother's house?' *And your mother's fence?*

'Yes,' Joel sighed, rubbing the back of his neck as if it ached. Maddie fought back the impulse to rub it for him. He looked so damnably attractive that her heart cried a little. 'And she plans to come up and live in it quite soon.' Maddie's ears perked up. There was that tone in his voice that led her to think he wasn't very happy over his mother's trip. And here was her chance!

'You know,' she started out conversationally, 'with your mother coming, and school about to start next door, and all, you really ought to consider finding a more isolated place to work.'

His head came up, and for the first time that night he smiled at her.

'Would you be interested——' she began, and then rephrased the question. 'There's a fine old house on the lake that's come on the market,' she said cautiously. 'Plenty of room, plenty of solitude, and it can be had— well, for a song, so to speak. For a writer looking for seclusion, this one could just hit the spot.'

'I might be interested,' Joel drawled, and his eyes bored holes in her. 'Not without seeing it, of course. I don't buy pigs in pokes.'

'No, of course not,' Maddie returned. Houses had been sold and fortunes in commissions made based on less than this! But a good salesperson never presses beyond a certain point. Silence descended on the pair of them again. Maddie wetted her dry lips, and searched for another subject, nursing her fledgling glee behind a solemn face. A fat profit from the sale, and he'd be twenty miles away! Who could ask for a sweeter deal?

'How is your writing going?'

It was the wrong subject. Joel frowned and ran a hand up through the hair on the side of his head. 'Not well,' he sighed. 'I need some inspiration. Or maybe there's just too much going on around this darn place.'

'There, just what I mentioned,' she suggested with her tongue in her cheek, 'A really isolated house. There are two hundred and seventy-four islands in Lake Winnipesauki, and a great many of them have houses on them. You couldn't ask for more isolation. The Murchison place would be just right for you. Of course, when I said you could have it for a song I meant—relatively. It's a very big estate.'

'What is this I hear?' Joel enquired. 'The mating cry of the real-estate salesman?'

'Salesperson,' she snapped. 'Think how much better off you would be, on an island all your own, far away from poky neighbours and their cats! Why, you and Bluebeard could have a ball! You should hear this street when the school opens in the fall. Automobiles, delivery vans, kids yelling and screaming—it's simply awful! And miles away, should your mother think to come up for the summer!'

'And you know just the house that would suit me. Isn't that convenient!' He shifted position, crossing one leg over the other. What big feet he has, Maddie thought. Think how tall he would be if there wasn't so much folded under!

'I'll check it out with Henri,' she suggested, trailing a little more bait in front of him. 'To be sure it's available.'

Like any shark, Joel bit—but at the wrong bait. 'Henri?' he asked aggressively. 'Who's Henri?' He grounded both feet with a thump and leaned forward in her direction as if he were about to spring.

Maddie shifted uneasily, leaning back against the padded arm of the sofa, wishing she were somewhere else entirely.

'Henri,' she explained. 'Henri LeFleur, my boss at the real estate office.'

'And that's all he is?' Those noble eyebrows were raised again. Caesar couldn't have done better, she told herself. What is *wrong* with this man!

'Well,' she said guardedly, 'that's *one* of the things he is.'

He started to say something else, but at that moment Tante Marie came through from the kitchen, her face alight. 'Ah, you two found something nice to talk about,

I see. Well, come on. I thought the kitchen would be best. It's only a light supper snack, you know.'

The pair of them followed Tante into the kitchen, Maddie tagging along far enough behind to be out of reach. As they went through the swinging door Mehitabel came down the stairs, started to join them, then noted the man in the procession. The cat arched his back and hissed, backing slowly away.

'Isn't that strange?' Tante Marie commented. 'I've never seen him do *that* before. Not when his supper dish is in the kitchen. What do you suppose is wrong, Madeleine?'

'Something he ate, no doubt,' Maddie replied. Another of the Biblical dicta handed down in the Charbonneau family. *A soft answer turneth away wrath.* If Tante Marie really knew how that man had treated our cat last week, there'd be fur flying from here to Montreal!

The little supper snack proved to be typical of Tante Marie. Just something picked up out of leftovers. You bet! Hot soup, homemade, followed by steak fillets, potatoes au gratin, Brussels sprouts, peas and carrots, and hot bread. Maddie surveyed the table and shook her head ruefully. There was no way to fight it; people who came late to Tante Marie's house *must* be hungry! The eleventh commandment in her great-aunt's upbringing, installed in her back in rural Quebec.

'So Joel was telling me that his writing isn't going well,' said Tante Marie after the soup was disposed of. 'What he needs is some inspiration.'

'I don't think I can help,' Maddie said politely, all the while thinking what a lot of information was exchanged in that few minutes at the kitchen door. Or have these two been conniving behind my back for a longer time than that? 'What sort of inspiration are you looking for, Mr Fairmont?'

'Call me Joel,' he insisted. 'It's hard to explain. I'm writing a—well, a historical romance, and——'

'Ah, one of those,' Maddie said sweetly. 'Best-seller types? Five hundred pages of passion? Bodice-ripping! Rape among the Rutabagas?'

'Madeleine!' Tante Marie was so upset she spilled her tea, and on her third-best tablecloth to boot.

'Well, it's true, Tante,' Maddie insisted. 'That's what goes on the best-seller lists. Times have changed, love. Didn't you ever hear of S.E.X. when you were young?' She spelled the letters out, rather than saying the word.

'We heard,' said Tante through clenched teeth. 'But not in books. And we certainly didn't talk about it at the dinner-table. I fear I've done badly in bringing you up, Madeleine Annette Charbonneau!'

And that does it, Maddie winced. The fat's in the fire when she calls me *that*! 'I'm sorry,' she mumbled, not meaning a word of it. The big man beside her at the table grinned. She kicked at his shin, forgetting she had left her shoes in the living-room. The pain was its own punishment. He hardly seemed to notice.

'That's better,' Tante Marie proclaimed. 'We all make slips in our manners now and then, Joel. We must excuse the young.'

'Yes, of course,' he said unctuously, but Maddie noted that he drew his leg out of her reach as he said it.

'Now I'm sure that Madeleine can help you with your research,' Tante continued, not noticing all the byplay beneath her table. 'And it just happens that she has Monday free.'

'But, Tante——' Maddie protested.

'And besides, she needs someone to accompany her,' her aunt continued, as relentlessly as a steamroller flattening a new construction area. 'And I'm sure there'll be something of what you need down at the Weirs.'

'Oh, there surely will,' Maddie added sarcastically, with her fingers crossed. 'Down on the boardwalk I'm sure we'll find just what Mr Fairmont—Joel—needs to inspire him.'

'The Weirs?' he queried.

'A place called Weir Beach,' Tante explained. 'It's a narrow channel between Lake Winnipesauki and Paugus Bay. The Indians used to put nets out in the channel to catch the fish. And sometimes they would build traps. A part of New Hampshire's history. I'm sure you'll enjoy all that.'

'Yes, I'm sure he will too,' Maddie agreed, crossing fingers on *both* hands. 'Maybe we could make it a double project—Joel? We could take a ride out to Glory Island and look at the Murchison estate?'

'Why, how exciting!' Tante Marie gushed. 'I saw it once, years ago. They say it was haunted, and——'

'Tante!' The old lady gulped as she gave Maddie a stricken look.

'Have I spoiled it with old wives' tales?' her aunt asked, with a quiver in her voice.

'Not at all,' Joel assured her. 'Haunted, huh? I've always had an interest in haunted houses. We'll go Monday. That's four days from now, right?'

Just like that, Maddie thought. The big old male decision-maker! Maybe I should stand up and make a curtsy? Or worse, maybe I'll sell him the damn house, haunts and all!

The rest of the evening passed quickly. Tante was tired, and left Maddie to wash up. She hadn't expected Joel to participate. He didn't. Just as soon as the old lady was out of the room the pair of them were back on war footing.

'You don't *have* to come,' she insisted as she escorted him to the back door.

'Yes, I do,' he said grimly. 'Your great-aunt will have a fit if I don't.'

'Well, I don't look forward to it being any barrel of fun either,' she said glumly. 'I don't like you, and you don't like me, and there's no use struggling with it.'

'Maybe that's not entirely true about us not liking each other,' said Joel over his shoulder as he got up. 'One of the disadvantages of having a boy next door is that the truth sometimes eludes you.' He stepped out into the night and went over to his own house, whistling.

'Having a *disagreeable* boy next door,' Maddie muttered the qualifier to herself as she went at the dishes. 'How in the name of all that's holy am I going to be able to put up with him for a full day?'

Mehitabel, who had sneaked into the kitchen when Tante Marie left, rubbed against her leg and purred.

'I know,' Maddie told her cat, 'you need to go out and see what's cooking tonight? Keep away from that black Persian up on the next block. She's already had three litters of pure white kittens!'

Mehitabel, who knew more about genetics than that, purred again, and scratched at the screen door.

CHAPTER FIVE

'WHY DON'T you give me the local lecture?' Joel suggested as they turned off the highway in the direction of Weir Beach.

Madeleine muffled a sigh. Monday had come despite her prayers. Joel had arrived with his Chrysler LeBaron convertible. When she added the cost of that car on to the Mustang he had previously driven, the price of the Murchison mansion went up ten per cent in her scheming mind.

She had dressed carefully; neither too radically or too conservatively. A loose pair of dark blue trousers. A lightweight white blouse which buttoned down the front. The whole worn over a soft white cotton teddy, and everything buttoned to the very top. Let him make something out of that, she thought vindictively. The eager desire to make a sale and get rid of him warred with her nervous fear of being alone with him for an entire day, and she suffered from the combat.

Because it was to be an outdoor day she had brushed her hair to a frazzle, pulled it back tightly away from her face, and fastened it in a ponytail, using rubber bands to hold it in place. A broad-brimmed straw hat perched on top of her head, and in her shoulder bag were the essentials for a 'wild day at the beach'. One compact, a packet of tissues, and the tiny crumpled bikini, just in case.

'There's nothing much to say,' Madeleine told Joel, very subdued for a Charbonneau. 'We're going north along a chain of lakes. The one at Laconia is called Opechee Bay. It's connected by a small river to Paugus Bay, and that's connected, through the Weirs, to Lake Winnipesauki. If you were to turn around and go south you'd find the entire chain of lakes ends up as the source of the Merrimac River.' And you look so—manly this morning, and for some reason I'm not sure that I want you to move away from McGrath Street, Mr Joel Fairmont, she thought. Maybe I'm suffering from a vitamin deficiency?

'But Winnipesauki is the biggest?'

'Of course. Something like seventy-two square miles of water.' She had been saying this for years, but suddenly it sounded peculiar. 'I don't believe I've ever seen square water,' she added. He chuckled.

'Turn right here,' she directed. 'Down the hill on Lakeside Avenue. And slowly. Pedestrians have the absolute right of way.'

'Now that's unusual,' commented Joel. 'In Boston pedestrians don't have any rights at all.'

'Huh!' she snorted. 'I went to school in Boston. I thought being a pedestrian was against the law!'

'And where do I park?' He had come almost to a stop, and the cars behind were making caustic horn noises. The entire avenue was lined on both sides by parking meters.

'Not here,' she advised. 'These meters run from half an hour to two hours. This is the Coney Island of New Hampshire, you know.' He drove slowly on down towards the two-block centre of activity, past the

Veterans' Building with its cannon outside, up towards the Arcades and the Bumper Car building.

'That's where I used to work when I was in High School,' Maddie told him proudly. 'I was a change girl in the Arcade. No, keep going, but slowly. The Methodist Church maintains an all-day car park up the hill.'

'Where do I turn?'

'On Church Street, where else? Just before that restaurant and arcade.'

Joel managed to turn through a sea of pedestrians, tourists all, and entered the almost-empty car park. Behind them, down the hill, came the deep tone of a locomotive, almost immediately suppressed by the foghorn roar of a ship's horn. He turned around excitedly in his seat, but could see nothing. Like a little boy, Maddie told herself. But such a big little boy.

Joel caught her staring at him, and the boyish grin disappeared. What replaced it was—what? A *wolfish* grin? Madeleine huddled as far over in the seat as she could go.

'You were a change girl?' he asked. Smooth, teasing tones, almost mesmerising. There was no room left on the seat into which she might squeeze, and she was so dazed she didn't even think to open the door and get out.

'Yes,' she told him firmly. 'I worked all through high school, except in the basketball season.' And then she flipped down the door handle and stepped, trembling, out into the car park.

Joel was around the car before she had adequately settled her mind, and offered her a hand. She refused by subterfuge, using both hers to set her straw hat in place and tie the little ribbon. So by the time he *did* take her hand and towed her out to the pavement, she was as calm as one could expect, for a girl who had just faced a startling revelation. There was warmth in a simple thing like holding his hand. Comfort from a point of contact. No wild stars revolving in the skies; no great and sudden surge of passion. Just a comfort. There are times, she told herself, when he can be sweet enough to eat!

'That hat's not fair,' Joel protested as he urged her down the hill, his eyes glistening at the sight of the diesel railroad locomotive pulling slowly into view from the west.

The hat was a problem, Maddie knew, as she used her free hand to keep it on. The wind was brisk on the lake, swirling little dust spirals off the boardwalk. Gulls were drilling by platoons just off-shore, diving in the only areas the power boats had left free. And off in the distance the white gleaming shape of the motor ship *Mount Washington* was just coming in view, all two hundred and thirty feet of excursion vessel sparkling in the morning sun.

Joel came to a stop at the foot of the hill, and Maddie finally caught up with him and her breath. 'What did you mean about my hat?' she panted.

'Your hat?' he said. 'If a man had a notion to kiss you he'd hardly be able to with that thing on your head.'

'Then a man hadn't better get such notions,' she snapped indignantly. 'You're altogether too free with your kisses, Mr Fairmont!' It felt better to have something to fight about. A little honest anger did a great deal to remove those strange feelings she had suffered in the last half-hour.

'Well, aren't we the little puritan?' he chuckled. 'I thought I left that all behind me in Massachusetts.'

'How would I know?' she huffed. 'Flatlanders do crazy things—we all know that. Do you plan to stand here all day?'

'I'm waiting for the traffic to slow.' Joel gestured up the street, where a round two dozen cars were slowly moving through the crowds. 'This may not be Boston, but I don't want to get run down.'

'You could wait for ever,' she snapped, tugging him along with her as she stepped out between the double white stripes. Immediately all the cars came to a halt. He looked at her, puzzled.

'I told you,' she lectured, as if talking to a delinquent child, 'pedestrians have the absolute right of way.'

'I don't believe this. My *friends* won't believe this.' He walked slowly, enjoying the grandeur of being king of the street. 'Whoever thought up this idea?'

'Chamber of Commerce,' she told him. 'Look, when people walk through the centre of the town it's possible they might stop here and there to buy something. People *driving* through are just trying to get someplace else. We don't need to encourage them to take their money elsewhere. But move along, Mr Fairmont. The railroad doesn't believe in the same rules about pedestrians.'

Joel took a quick look around and hustled. The locomotive, with three cars attached, had begun to move again, along the tracks laid at the lakeward side of the road. A half-mile or more of boardwalk paralleled the railroad tracks. Half-way down the boardwalk a tiny old-fashioned railroad station was the centre of tourist attention.

'What the devil did you put in this lunch basket?' he quipped, hefting the lunch that Tante Marie had packed. 'You went shopping at the supermarket?' Maddie struggled with her hat while trying to look up at him. Everything he said had some underlying meaning to it, and she wasn't about to commit herself without seeing his expression.

'No,' she said cautiously. 'I haven't been shopping this week. I brought some things home from the deli, though. Why do you ask?'

'Oh, nothing important,' he shrugged. 'I guess I'm a grocery clerk at heart.'

His regal tone was just enough to set Maddie off. 'You don't have to be snobbish,' she raged at him. 'There's nothing wrong with being a grocery clerk, providing you work hard at it and do your best. Supermarkets are very important to our civilisation.'

Joel shook his head, and his hand automatically went up and through his hair. 'Well,' he drawled, 'I never thought about it that way.'

'You should,' she snapped. 'You know, one of the things wrong with you is——'

'I suppose there's no way I can stop you telling me?' he interrupted, smiling.

'No way,' Maddie returned firmly. 'Arrogance, that's your problem. Just because you're a successful writer, you look down your nose at grocery clerks! The secret to a happy life is to do the best you can at whatever station in life you're called to!' She looked down to find that her hands were clenched into hard tight fists, restrained under her breasts, as if she meant to club him. And Tante would never approve of that, her conscience lectured. She relaxed her fingers. Arrogant man!

Joel Fairmont was all boy now, hustling her along with a vicelike grip on her elbow, heading for the station. To their left the land came to an abrupt end in a little cliff, dropping off to water level, where two piers and a rats'-nest of interwoven marinas provided shelter for a multitude of boats of all kinds. And by this time the *Mount Washington* had docked, and hordes of tourists flooded the ramp that led up to the boardwalk.

'Crazy,' he said in admiration. 'They don't have anything like *this* in Boston.'

Maddie laughed. 'Boston harbour's polluted so badly that even the fish are walking; up here we go to a lot of trouble to keep the Lake clean. It's our bread and butter. Let's start the research for your book over there at the tables.'

She led him around behind the railroad station to where a small area, an extension of the boardwalk, was equipped with benches and picnic tables and a tiny grill. They were lucky; one of the tables in the shade was empty. As Maddie slid on to the bench Joel stopped by the grill and ordered for them.

When his coffee mug was empty and her Pepsi almost gone Joel came back to the main subject. 'Research,' he said pulling a little notebook out of his pocket. 'Where?'

'Right here,' she said, pointing. Directly in front of them couples and threesomes were parading up and down the boardwalk in a slow, ritualised walk, to see and be seen.

'My God!' he sighed. Maddie agreed with him. There were tall ones and short ones, wide ones and thin ones, in all manner of dress and undress. Men and women, as God had made them. A woman of perhaps forty, hardly five feet tall, and wider than that, a size fourteen lady in a size ten bikini, every inch of her rolling in different directions as she walked.

'Got that down?' teased Maddie. Joel glared at her and slowly put his pen away.

'Then how about that pair?' she suggested. Two stylishly plump girls, perhaps seventeen or eighteen, both equipped with pneumatic figures fore and aft, strolling along with exaggerated hip movements in bikinis and high heels.

'My Gawd!' he repeated.

'Better close your eyes before you burn out your eyeballs,' Madeleine said sarcastically. He snapped his head around and stared at her as if she were some stranger. 'Me,' she coaxed. 'Madeleine Charbonneau, you remember?'

'I remember,' he replied slowly. 'You're the jealous one, I believe.'

'Jealous of them?' she snorted. 'And there's no use licking your lips. There's no bodice-ripping allowed around here. That's what the policeman at the corner is for. This is strictly a family entertainment area!'

'You *are* jealous!' he crowed. 'Maddie Carbonneau, jealous of a couple of high school kids!'

'Charbonneau,' she corrected with an icy coolness of which Tante Marie would have been proud. 'Got it all down? Isn't that the kind of research you need for your book?'

'Hell, no,' Joel snapped. 'Let's go someplace else. Where does that train go?'

'Nowhere,' she retorted. The three-car train was filling rapidly, as the tourists off the boat transferred.

'Now I know you're a fruitcake,' he muttered. 'A railroad that goes nowhere?'

Maddie shook her head as she considered him. A writer with no imagination? The wind had tilted her hat up over one eye. She used the time of adjustment to think it out. There was definitely something wrong in all this. 'Are you sure you're a writer?' she asked cautiously.

Joel almost choked on the last of his drink. She leaned over to pat his back. 'Of course I'm a writer,' he growled when his throat finally cleared. 'What's that got to do with trains that don't go anywhere?'

'The train is run by a hobby group,' she explained. 'It runs—oh, just for the hell of it. It goes west from here almost to the town of Meredith, where they have a little railroad yard. Then it comes back through the Weir and goes almost to Lakeport, where they stop in the middle of a trestle, switch the engine to the other end of the train, and come back.'

'You're right,' he chuckled, 'it doesn't go anyplace. Lord, what a rip-off!'

'It's not, you know,' she said thoughtfully. 'There are lots of times in life when the arriving isn't half as important as the going there.'

Joel leaned across the rough pine table and grasped her two hands in one, with a gentle squeeze. 'Philosophy?' he queried solemnly. 'Perhaps you're right. I'll remember that. Maybe I'll put it in my book.'

'You're welcome,' she smiled. 'How many books have you written?'

It would be hard to say that a man so heavily tanned could blush, but for just a second Maddie thought he had. At least he looked a little embarrassed. 'Counting this one?' he asked.

'Yes, if you want to.'

'In that case, one,' he returned. Maddie was so startled she jerked away from him, spilling the residue of her drink down the front of her trousers.

'One? This is the—you haven't done any *others* but this one?'

'You've got it,' he grinned. 'I've come to a change of life. Put everything behind me, and starting on a new career.'

'But—but,' she stammered, 'I've known a writer or two, Joel.' The name came easily to her lips, something she hardly noticed, although he did. 'You surely must know, even if your first book is a success, it will be years before you make any money!'

'I'll survive,' he assured her. 'Grandfather left me well fixed. You don't think it's a wise move?'

'I've never had time to think of things like that,' she shrugged. 'Jobs are a necessity, and that's the only way you keep alive. I've been working since I was fourteen.'

It wasn't often that Madeleine felt sorry for herself, and this little performance had stolen up on her unawares. But I won't cry, she told herself. Women with responsibilities don't cry! She sniffed a couple of times and turned away from him so he would not see her knuckle brushing the single tear away.

'So you've come to a change of life?' she added brightly. 'I didn't realise you were that old.'

'I'm thirty-three years old, but age has nothing to do with it,' Joel said grimly. He stood up and pulled her up with him. She clutched at her hat. Hats were easier to control than hearts, she told herself. And for some reason her heart was giving trouble!

'The boat's down there.' Madeleine gestured towards the down-ramp, and the floating docks, where dozens of small boats were sheltered in individual slips. 'Why don't we go and look at the house?'

His hand was under her elbow as she stumbled down the wide ramp, cursing the folly that had led her to change to two-inch heels. So I'll be taller, she had thought that morning. So how tall will you be if you wind up in a pratfall? her conscience laughed.

She looked up at Joel to see if he were paying attention. His head was thrown back and he was staring out into the broad reach of the lake. The wind ruffled his hair but was ignored. He was every inch a Viking, looking for his ship, for lands to conquer, for towns to pillage, for women to——

'Around here someplace?' he asked loudly. The wind, down here at lake-level, made normal speech impossible. The snarl of half a hundred inboard and outboard motorboats did little to ease the situation. Maddie slipped out from under his hand and skipped to get ahead of him as they walked down the length of the floating dock.

Henri's runabout was a sixteen-foot outboard speedster. Half the length of the hull was open cockpit. A small canvas shelter served as wheelhouse. The forward deck was covered—mahogany on a fibre-glass hull! In keeping with its owner's occupation, the little craft was named *It's A Deal!*

'You know how to operate this?' Joel called as Maddie jumped down into the cockpit and turned around to face him. He was not exactly enthusiastic, she could tell. But she had become accustomed to that sort of thing over many years of experience with Doubting Thomases.

'I have a Coast Guard certificate,' she announced grandly. 'Are you coming or not?'

'I'm coming,' grumbled Joel. The boat swayed as his weight hit the deck. 'I don't know why, but I'm coming.'

Maddie moved into the wheelhouse, checked all the instruments, used her nose to detect any fuel leaks, then hit the starter button. The two outboard Hondas grumbled, spat a couple of times, then settled down into a smooth purr.

Without instruction Joel cast off the stern lines, then scrambled forward. At her signal he took in the bow lines, then gave the boat a little push away from the dock with his foot. They came out of the little slip sedately, paying due attention to all the rules, and being wary of all the idiots who were zooming in and out of the area regardless of rules, sending rooster-sprays of fresh water high in the sky.

'Are all these people mad?' he shouted at Maddie as he struggled back into the wheelhouse. She gestured towards the pile of life-jackets under the seat, and pantomimed the order to put them on. 'Who, me?' he roared.

Maddie nodded, and pointed to her own. Joel shook his head in disgust, but complied. And then he came back to stand beside her, his shoulder just behind hers, his feet spread apart to accommodate the waves. They bounced over the wake of one of the racing boats. The movement forced her off balance, and she banged against him. His arm went around her shoulders to steady her. It felt—comfortable.

She kept her eyes open as they moved out into the channel around the west end of Governor's Island, following along like a little splinter in the track of the *Mount Washington*. The big ship, having loaded itself with a new batch of tourists, was ploughing along at fourteen knots on its way to Center Harbor. But when the *Washington* turned west into the channel between Bear Island and Meredith Neck, Maddie kept straight ahead through the little channels between Mark and Bear, Mink and Camp, Jolly and Kineo, until they were among the Forty Islands. She slowed the engines and turned into the concealed cove that lay in the shadow of Glory Island's south shore.

'Why here?' asked Joel, moving with her to help handle the heavy mooring.

'I thought you knew. I planned to take you up to the Murchison house. This entire island is part of the estate—acres of solitude.'

'Well,' Joel sighed, 'I should have known, I suppose. All right, lady, take me up to the Murchison house.'

Maddie had been concentrating on the course as the channel twisted in and out between huge rocks. For just a moment she flashed a look up into his eyes. They were gleaming, sparkling, and he was laughing! She snapped back to her piloting job, but her mind raced at miles per second. All those complaints, and still he smiles? Smell the rat, Madeleine Charbonneau? Go carefully!

For another five minutes all Maddie's concentration was required to keep the boat off the sandy bottom and the rocks. She gave a sigh of relief as they came around the last turn in the approach channel, where the cove widened into a beautiful pool. A decrepit wooden wharf barely managed to hold its head up out of the water at the far side. Maddie shifted into neutral and the little runabout glided across the glass-still water.

Joel went up in the bow without command, standing casually with legs spread apart, holding the lines in hand.

As they came closer he kicked the little bumper-pad over the port side to avoid scratching the little craft's paint.

When he dropped his hand, Maddie shifted into reverse. A storm of water surged up under the propellers, and the runabout came to a shuddering halt, inches from the pier. Joel stepped across and had two half-hitches around the bollard before Maddie could think to tell him. She shook her head as she cut the engine. There was a great deal—a very great deal about this man that she didn't know—yet!

'You're not coming ashore?' he called from the wharf. He caught the stern lines and made them fast while waiting for an answer.

'Tante Marie made us up a big lunch,' she returned. 'It's quite a walk to the house. I thought we might just stay aboard and eat before we go up. Unless you have an objection?'

'Who, me?' he grinned as he jumped back on to the boat. 'Why would *I* argue?'

Maddie felt uneasy. As long as the boat was moving she had felt safe, but now it seemed that previous rules no longer applied. He was grinning, true, but with the grin of a wolf on the hunt.

More than once, in her chequered past, she had found a man who disturbed her. But with her athletic skills, she had always found enough physical strength to stay clear. But this man—lord, not only was she afraid, but her muscles had turned to jelly. Whatever it was Joel wanted, she wanted too.

A very confused young lady sat down and unpacked the bag of food. Fried chicken—not the commercial kind, but Tante Marie's own speciality, light and crisp and tasty, well matched by the little plastic container of

salad. Maddie's hand shook as she sat down on the ban-
quette and fished out the napkins and plastic cutlery.

Joel was standing too close—far too close. She stirred
uneasily, and shifted away from him. But not far enough.
The big grin was warning enough to snap her to attention. She struggled to get up, but he was astride her
recumbent form, and there was no escape.

He was so close to her that Maddie could hardly focus
on his face. There was an insistent desire deep in her
brain. Close your eyes and see what happens!

'You are one crazy mixed-up kid,' murmured Joel,
relenting enough for her to stand up. It was her mistake.
No sooner had she gained her feet than he swept her up
in one of his patented embraces, wrapping her up as if
he had ten octopus-arms. Well, she told herself, there
you are. It's no use fighting him, Maddie, because you
don't want to!

It was a relief not to struggle. She relaxed all her
muscles, let her weight hang on his arms, against his
warm, strong body. Her mind stopped playing like a
squirrel in a revolving cage. There was no reason to
reason, no place for decisions. No cautions about how
she hated him, how he irritated her, how she—loved him?
Nothing seemed important. Just the warmth, the
comfort, the soft, fluttering touch of his lips to hers.

For what seemed to be long minutes she hung there,
feeling the slow increase of tension, the building of
passions, the steady change of mood as his hands untied
her life-jacket, unbuttoned her blouse, and went ex-
ploring along the top curves of her teddy.

In another moment they were down on the floor of
the cockpit, Joel's hand a flame as it closed on her breast,
inciting her to riotous response that overwhelmed

her careful calm mind. 'Don't—don't—don't——'
Madeleine panted, her mind unclear.

Joel paused. 'Don't what?' he asked. There was des-
peration in his voice, but she could not hear it.

'Don't stop,' she sighed, squirming against him,
pushing his hand back down to her breast. 'Dear lord,
don't stop——'

She had no way to measure what was happening. She
had had her share of groping dates in high school, but
lately there had been a dearth. All the young reliable
ones had married; the men who were left uncaught were
not worth catching. But what all this passion might have
led to never came to pass. The boat jolted, swung wildly,
and began to bounce against the wharf.

They broke apart and sprang to their feet. The sky
was black, thunderstorm-black. With an economy of
motion Joel shovelled Maddie back into her life-jacket
as she fumbled for the right buttons to turn on the ship-
board radio. It was already tuned to the Coast Guard
frequency. With care she re-tuned and turned up the
volume. The station was broadcasting a recorded
message, repeating it over and over without pause.
'Emergency storm warning, all sections of Lake
Winnipesauki. All craft take shelter!'

CHAPTER SIX

'WHAT DO WE do now?' Joel shouted to Madeleine. The rising storm was both loud and imminent. 'Run for home?'

Maddie looked up at the clouds and shivered. The thunder heads towered high in the sky. The wind gusted from the south east, over the tops of the Belnap Mountains, screaming across the open lake, and battering the low, exposed shore of Glory where they were anchored. Only the small shelter of the cove helped them. And storms on shallow lakes, she knew, were twice as dangerous as those on the open ocean. Already the boat had risen six inches or more, as the storm winds relentlessly pushed water into the constricted throat of the anchorage.

'No!' she yelled back. 'It's too dangerous on the lake. Help me make the runabout fast, and then let's find some shelter!'

Joel was a man of quick reflexes. While Maddie fumbled around in the cockpit trying to decide what to take, he had already doubled up both fore and aft lines, and was offering his hand to her. With the boat bouncing and twisting under the advance party of the storm, she needed the help.

'This won't do much good,' he said, pointing to the boat. 'There's nothing to keep it from smashing up against the dock!'

'I know,' Maddie called back. 'I put the anchor out to starboard, but—lord, Henri will kill me if his boat is wrecked!'

'I want to meet this guy Henri,' yelled Joel as he cupped her elbow and urged her up the twisting path. Glory was a small island, low on the south side, slanting gradually upwards to a grassy plateau, with sharp cliffs on the north. The house stood at the edge of that plateau, looking out over the cliffs. Pine trees and oaks provided a windbreak, but the trees had only a tenuous hold on the thin soil, and became a part of the danger when gale winds snatched them out by the roots and used them as battering rams.

They struggled upward for about ten yards before he pulled Maddie to a halt in the shelter of a trio of huge boulders. 'Give me that stuff you're carrying,' Joel shouted directly into her ear. She passed the bag to him gladly. Battling with the wind was not part of her training cycle, and she was already breathless. And those shoes with the two-inch heels—what a stupid choice *that* had turned out to be! She grabbed at his strong arm for support and danced on one foot as she removed the offending half-boots. He grinned as he snatched them from her and shoved them into his shirt pockets, toes down. 'Ready?' he asked. She took a deep breath and nodded.

The going was easier on the next segment of the trail. In its windings back and forth the path had turned away from the wind, and the trees provided a better shelter. It had been a long time since Maddie had gone barefoot, however, and the path was not smooth. No sooner had they come to the next turn in the trail than her foot impacted on the sharp edge of a flint, and blood began to flow. Not much blood, and in her state of excitement, fighting against nature, she hardly noticed. But Joel did. Little specks of red trailed them, and he picked it up.

And then he picked *her* up, swinging her around and into his arms, one hand at her back, the other under her knees. He stopped. Her ear was close to his mouth; at least they could communicate. 'I've seen this done in a hundred movies,' he told her, juggling her weight to find an easier carry-point. 'How come you're so heavy?'

'Put me down!' she yelled at him. The excitement, the danger, the clash of thunder, all conspired to tease her tense anger. 'You can't even get the hero part right, can you!'

'Disillusioned?' laughed Joel. But he *did* set her down, and then bent over for leverage and threw her up on his shoulder in the fireman's carry. With her head upside down, bobbing over his back, and one hand and one foot in his grasp, making it impossible for her to move, she was trapped, angry, humiliated—and being carried in perfect safety up the side of a long long hill. So why fight? Maddie thought. If he wants to be a hero, why should I struggle for the right to walk barefoot up a rocky hill? It all seemed so logical that she relaxed and let the world happen.

Joel managed capably for another thirty or forty yards before the front line of the gale reached them. Beaten by the wind and the huge drops of water, he found them another niche between two rocks, set Maddie down with a groan of relief, then tucked her in close to him to provide all the shelter his frame would allow. They were soaked in an instant. The raindrops were so huge that they hit on the surrounding rocks and actually bounced back into the air, still in their spheroid form. The two huddled uncomfortably, heads down, as lightning splashed in every direction. Not more than a hundred yards away from them a tree that had the nerve to grow taller than its neighbours was suddenly split down the middle by a bolt. Maddie ducked her head into Joel's armpit; this was not the sort of bravery test she was best at. They could smell the smoke as the charred giant creaked and then fell.

The roll of thunder that followed immediately after the lightning flash was so loud that it shook the hill. And then, as fast as it had come up, that particular segment of the storm was swept away from them, headed across the lake towards Moltonborough. The silence was overwhelming. Somewhere up above them a couple of quails sounded their Bob-White call, as if the storm were over.

'There'll be more to come,' Maddie told Joel anxiously. 'Lots more! We have to find shelter and——'

'I know,' he replied. 'But take a quick look down at the cove.' They had zigged and zagged a couple of times, and were now back to a point where the anchorage was in view. Maddie wiped the water out of her eyes and stared. The runabout, Henri's pride and joy, had been snatched away from the wharf and smashed across a pair of rocks on the other side of the anchorage, its back broken.

'Oh, me!' she muttered, her mind divorced from her voice, 'Thank God I brought the chicken with me!'

'Now that's the kind of girl I like,' laughed Joel. 'Get your priorities right! Rescue the food, and forget the million-dollar yacht!'

'Oh!' She blanched at the thought. 'Surely not a million——?'

'No. Probably about a thousand dollars a foot,' he corrected himself. 'Hardly twenty, or twenty-five thousand dollars. A drop in the bucket.'

'That depends on whose bucket you're talking about,' she moaned. 'That's what I make for a whole year's work.'

'Yeah, well, we've got more to worry about than that,' he told her. 'Let me see that foot of yours.'

She turned around and held it up for inspection. He handled the foot like a farrier shoeing a horse. The rain continued, reduced to a fine mist, but over towards the top of Gunstock Mountain Maddie could see additional towering thunderheads, with their promise of more to come.

'Not bad,' commented Joel as he dropped her foot to the ground. 'Just a small cut. But you shouldn't walk on it and it wouldn't help to try to bandage it right this minute, so—upsy-daisy, little girl.'

'Don't you wish I were!' she snorted. 'A *little* girl, I mean.'

'Good lord,' he laughed as he swung her back up over his shoulder, 'what an inferiority complex you have! You're just exactly the size girl with whom I'd like to be shipwrecked on a deserted island.' The words sounded so comforting that Maddie smiled, even as he began to jog uphill, sending her bouncing and swaying—and smiling—towards the top of the hill.

They came upon the house suddenly. The trail curved to the right through the pinewoods, made a sharp jog to the left, and there it was before them. It wasn't exactly the view that a good salesperson would want, but even in the world's drenched condition the Murchison mansion was impressive. The central core of the building was three floors high, built of local stone. The two wings were stone at the ground floor, with a superstructure in wood, of Gothic design. Two wooden towers stood guard at the far ends of each wing, towering above the rest of the house by a good fifteen feet. A huge front porch led to a pair of equally huge front doors. A cluster of ancient oak trees surrounded the whole. 'Holy cow!' muttered Joel. And then the rains returned.

'Run!' he ordered. Maddie hesitated for a second. A broad expanse of grass separated them from shelter, and the storm was grumbling at them. 'It's safer to run than wait here,' he coaxed tugging at her arm. A massive stroke of lightning lit the sky to the south. She lowered her head and ran.

They thundered up on to the veranda in a dead heat. The old boards of the steps shook as they bounded up to safety. The veranda roof leaked, but only in a couple of places. As they huddled up against the front door the rain pulverised the landscape, but they were out of the storm's reach.

The excitement faded, replaced by the trembling torment of fear. Maddie struggled to breathe, nestling up against Joel's soaked shirt. Her leg muscles fluttered spasmodically. She hung on to him for support, dimly appreciating his strength. Moments later, her mind under control—if not her body—she moved slightly away and gave him a weak smile.

'The keys?' he asked. 'I do believe the damn door's solid oak!' He rattled the verdigris-stained knob a couple of times. Maddie had a million things she might have said, but what came out was a total surprise to both of them.

'It's a fine house,' she murmured. 'If you buy it you'll love it.'

'Always a salesman,' he laughed. 'Do I have to sign the papers before I can seek refuge? Where are the keys?'

'I—I think they're down in the boat,' she stammered. 'I—took the food and left my purse and the keys are in it, and I don't care if you never spend a penny for a house like this and—oh God, why am I babbling so?'

Joel pulled her gently back against his chest, holding her there with one hand behind her head, making soothing noises. 'There now, you don't have to be brave any more,' he murmured into her ear. 'The danger's past. Cry it all out, love.' Maddie leaned against him, borrowing from his strength, letting all her pride and prejudice slip away from her on the surface of the tears. Cold, wet through and through, tired, yet suddenly she felt warm and safe—and it was good to feel so.

'Now then, one more hair pin,' Joel coaxed cheerfully. He squatted down in front of the doorknob as she watched him pick the lock. The storm was raging on all sides, but in their little enclave it hardly seemed to matter. Some of his cheerfulness was catching. Maddie smiled as she fumbled in her hair for another pin.

The ancient lock squeaked a protest and then clicked open. The door swung silently back. Maddie hesitated. In the dim light of the afternoon the interior corridor looked dark, forbidding. Joel's arm came around her shoulder and ushered her across the threshold. 'After you, my love,' he urged. He didn't mean much by it, she told herself, but the words sent goose-bumps up her spine.

They were in the middle of a hall that stretched up through the full three floors. A huge glass dome, incredibly dirty, scattered little splatters of light across the black and white tessellated floor. Directly ahead of them a staircase in the grand manner curved gently as it climbed. It was guarded by two marble Spartan soldiers, both leaning on their spears.

'Great day in the morning,' Joel sighed in awe. 'It looks like some of those millionaire cottages down in Newport! You know, the tasty little beach houses with thirty-eight rooms and a two-acre lawn! Who was this Murchison fellow?'

'I don't really know,' Maddie replied as she walked to the exact centre of the hall and slowly turned around. 'Some railroad magnate from New York, back in the days of the robber barons. There's a sort of mystery about the house. He built it for his very young wife, and on the first night he was in the building he—somehow—fell down those stairs and broke his neck.'

'And the wealthy widow?'

'She went off to Europe on a grand tour, or something like that. Isn't this tremendous?'

Joel walked over to the first door on his right and opened it. 'Ah, the study,' he called over his shoulder. 'And a big fireplace, complete with logs. The first thing we both need to do is get dry. Why don't you scout around quickly and see if you can find us some clothing—or blankets, that would do. I'll get the fire going.'

'I—don't think I'll have any luck.' It was something Maddie didn't want to tell him, but confession could hardly be avoided. Her voice seemed to have acquired a squeak. 'Nobody's lived in this place for the past twenty-eight years.'

He was down on one knee in front of the fireplace, and looked up with that big grin on his face. 'Not exactly a saleable house, is it? But I like it. Get going!'

Strangely angry again, Maddie turned on her heel and stalked up the stairs. He liked it? For every step her foot touched, the price of the house went up another five hundred dollars!

When Madeleine came back into the study Joel had a roaring fire going. She hurried across the room, dragging her trophy behind her. The room was responding to the fire, for which she was thankful. The old house had no central heating.

'What's that you trapped?' he asked, staring at the train she was towing behind her.

'It's all I could find,' she stammered. 'It's dark up there. But there were these curtains on the hall windows. They're made out of velvet, and there's a pair.'

She whirled the two curtains around in front of her, and Joel coughed as the dust from the old hangings spread through the room. 'Well,' she offered defiantly, 'it was all I could find. And I *did* shake them out before I brought them downstairs.'

'I'm not complaining,' he laughed. 'Come on, while the fire's still hot. Slip out of all that wet stuff and do yourself up in velvet!'

'Not here!' she stated flatly. 'I don't run peepshows!'

'If you're that sensitive, there are plenty of other rooms,' he drawled. 'But this is the only one with a warm fire. I think I'll just go ahead and——' His hand reached for his belt buckle.

'Don't you dare!' she shouted at him, and was instantly contrite. 'I—I'm sorry. But a real gentleman would leave me to the fire, and he'd go——'

'Out in the cold?' he chuckled. 'But I thought you'd already decided that I wasn't a real gentleman.'

'I might have been wrong,' she mumbled. It was probably the most insincere apology heard in the Lake area since the Civil War, but Joel grinned an acceptance anyway.

'I'll give you ten minutes,' he promised—or threatened—as he rubbed his hands one last time in front of the fire and headed for the hall.

Madeleine followed behind him—to be sure the door's closed, she told herself. He allowed her the honour. She limped back to the fire as fast as her battered feet would carry her. The blouse came off easily, but the teddy was plastered to her body, and peeling it off was like skinning an under-ripe banana. Both items fell to the floor and lay in their own little puddles. Her trousers and briefs quickly followed. She pirouetted in front of the flames a couple of times, revelling in the warmth, finger-brushing her hair to shake out the drops. Twice more for good luck, then she picked up the old curtain. It was almost six feet long, as befitting the big windows on the second floor. Another puff of dust assaulted her lungs.

It *had* to be shaken or beaten or washed again. Maddie backed away from the fire, aware for the first time that she was leaving a little trail of blood on the immaculate floor. But modesty was her first priority. With both hands on one end of the curtain she proceeded to give it a good shaking. So she made a beautiful picture standing naked in the firelight, gracefully swinging the length of velvet back and forth, when Joel came back in.

She was making too much noise for herself as she worked, humming a little 'happiness' song as she rhythmically flipped the velvet up and down. Strange— a mad storm, a wrecked boat, a stranded seafarer, a soaked girl—and still she was happy. It was a sensation she could not define. Madeleine Charbonneau was a long way from home, and she had just accepted things as they were. Until her little dance backed her up into Joel, and his big hands came around and cupped her breasts.

'Oh, no!' she screamed, and whirled away from him, pulling the curtain up in front of her for protection. 'No!' she repeated without the hysteria. 'You said ten minutes!'

'You've had fifteen,' he reported, consulting his wristwatch. 'Maybe more!' He shook the wrist wearing the watch. 'Damn thing is supposed to be waterproof. Would you beat that? I paid a fortune for that thing, and it's stopped!'

'You were watching,' she accused, managing to make a sarong out of her curtain without revealing too much flesh.

'Yes, I was,' he admitted, as if he were proud of the idea. 'You're a lovely lady, Madeleine!'

If he thought her attractive that might translate to *desirable*. And *that* Maddie was not about to accept. Better to be ugly and safe. 'I am not,' she muttered, backing away from him towards the fire.

'All right,' he agreed casually. 'I don't mean that you're the kind of girl who sets the world on fire. I just felt you deserved a compliment.'

It was just the touch Maddie wanted from him. Casual disinterest. And having got it so easily she was immediately peeved, and turned her back. Joel was too canny to put up with the snobbery. Her velvet sarong was long enough to accumulate a trailing train. Joel stepped on that train as she walked away. The knot under her breasts immediately dissolved, and her only covering fell to the floor.

She shrieked at him as she whirled and snatched it up again.

'I take it all back,' he laughed. 'You *could* set the world on fire!' She could see the hungry look in his eyes. Or perhaps it was only the flickering flame? Whatever, she no longer felt safe, but she *did* feel considerably happier. They joined forces, standing side by side in front of the fire, absorbing the warmth, but also falling into the hypnosis that is man's inheritance as he gazes into open flames.

Some minutes later Joel gave himself a shake and touched her shoulder. 'Let's get our things hung up here somehow so they'll dry,' he suggested. The mantel over the fireplace was long and wide and marble. It provided plenty of space for what little each of them had been wearing. He dumped his slacks, shirt, and shorts in an untidy heap. Maddie set her few articles out neatly, then impatiently rearranged his.

'You need a wife,' she told him. 'Sloppy here, sloppy at home. Or a housemaid.'

'Are you applying for the job?' he asked. She was staring into the fire when he spoke, and missed the look on his face. But it sounded facetious, so she treated it in that manner.

'I'd have to think it over,' she reported brightly. 'I have all my weekdays tied up. I might get a weekend or two loose from time to time? Maybe I could squeeze you

in, say, in September. I don't have my appointment cal-
endar with me at the moment.'

'What a shame,' he rumbled. 'But do keep me on your
list. Now, the question is, how do we get out of here?'

She shook her head in disgust and walked over to a
window. It looked out on to the path up which they had
come just an hour earlier. The rain was coming down
in torrents. The path ran like a river. Half a dozen trees
had been knocked down by the wind, others were still
swaying in the gusts. It was getting too dark to see as
far as the cove. Night was falling, and the storm looked
as if it might last the night.

'In this weather we haven't a prayer until morning,'
Maddie reported, with a little catch in her voice.

'That bothers you, spending a night with me?'

'No,' she said hurriedly. 'I can't say that I'm thrilled
about spending a night with you, but—— Tante Marie
will worry, you know. She's a great worrier. A great
eighty-five-year-old worrier.'

The grin disappeared from his face. 'You think a lot
of that lady, don't you?' He came over to join her at
the window, dropping one arm casually over her
shoulder. Without thinking she leaned back against him,
happy to draw on his strength again.

'Yes, very much. She's been the making of me. If it
hadn't been for Tante Marie I would have been foisted
off on Uncle Fred——'

'The police chief?' Joel interjected. 'What's so bad
about that?'

'Nothing really,' she said thoughtfully. 'But twenty-
five years ago he was just a patrolman, with six children
of his own, and things were pretty tight. Maybe I might
have grown up a better person for the competition,

but——' a little tearing sob broke in her throat '—but I'm happy Tante came for me. I'd do anything for that woman. Anything.'

'That's nice,' said Joel, and sounded as if he meant it. 'I'm my mother's only child, but I can't say that I had it as nice as you did.'

She craned her neck and stared up at him. 'No father?' she asked.

'No father,' he returned. 'Oh, I *had* a father, but he was too busy with his business to pay me any attention. He died when I was about fifteen. I think I might have missed the funeral if my mother hadn't reminded me.'

'That's an awful thing to say about your father!' She whirled around to face him, meaning to lecture, only to find herself trapped in his arms. For a moment they froze. 'No,' she whispered, 'don't!'

'Don't? I wasn't planning to do anything,' Joel returned gently. 'Not a thing.' His hands took her elbows and tethered her.

'Tell me about your father,' gasped Maddie, fighting back her own traitorous emotions.

'There's nothing to tell.' His face hardened as he spoke, almost as if he had turned to stone. 'He was completely absorbed in his business. I was a minor inconvenience. And when I refused to join the family corporation—well, that so upset him that he had a heart attack. And he added that to his list of *my* deficiencies——'

'You don't have any deficiencies,' she interrupted him with a startled intensity that she didn't know she possessed. Joel's hands squeezed her arms gently, reminding her of where she was and who *he* was. 'Well, outside of——'

'I know,' he sighed. 'You don't have to repeat them. Arrogance and—I know there's something else, but don't remind me. Now, let's see about that foot of yours.' Despite her protests he swept her up in the cradle of his arms and carried her over to the fire. Her excess velvet served as a cushion, protecting her from the cold marble floor. He squatted down beside her and had a look at her foot.

Maddie was content to sit in the warmth and watch him, silhouetted against the flame. When he got up and moved away she felt a little shiver of loneliness, even though he had only gone to the end of the mantel, where his shirt became a sacrificial victim. He tore off one of the tails and disappeared out into the hall. Moments later she heard the front door slam, and he came back with a soaking wet cloth and used it to bathe her foot.

'It's not bad,' he reported. 'Just a small cut, and I think I've got it clean.' The other shirt-tail became a bandage. He worked efficiently, neatly, as if he knew what he was doing. But that's his trademark, she told herself. A day ago—two days ago, the idea would have been annoying. Now there was just a touch of pleasure about it all. It was *good* to meet an efficient dependable man, instead of all the wimps she usually associated with. So he has a bad temper, she reasoned. Who doesn't? If anything, mine is worse than his and he isn't even French!

She squirmed around on her little cushion to find a more comfortable position, and found that he had established himself as a back-rest for her.

'The one thing I don't understand, Joel,' she sighed as she leaned back against his strength, 'is why and what you're doing now. Are you serious about this novel?'

The answer came with a little chuckle behind it. 'I thought so last week, Maddie. This week I seem to have acquired other priorities.' He paused and ruminated for a moment. 'Stupid, I guess, at thirty-three, but I'm conducting a protest against life. At least that's what my mother says.'

'She sounds like a very wise woman. Why?'

'Why is she wise?'

'No, why are you protesting?'

Joel thought that one over for another couple of minutes as the fire crackled at them, and one log spat out a glowing cinder. 'Because people wanted to force me into a kind of life I didn't want. I didn't want my wings clipped. But now——'

'Now?' she queried.

'Would you believe, I've had second thoughts,' he laughed. 'Like Bluebeard, I'm beginning to wonder if flying is all it's cracked up to be. And that's enough snooping, lady. Settle back and relax.'

'Well,' Joel interrupted Maddie's dream some thirty minutes later, 'it's getting dark, and you're the local expert. What do we do next?'

'I'm afraid there's nothing we can do tonight,' she sighed. 'The Coast Guard will be gathering a missing persons list tonight, but they won't be able to do any searching. If the storm is gone by morning, they'll have helicopters and patrol boats from the auxiliary out everywhere. It's a little too far to swim to the adjacent islands—a couple of miles, I would guess. We don't have a radio, we don't have a telephone——'

'And we don't even have electricity,' he chuckled. 'Lord, what a wreck of a house you're trying to unload on me, Maddie Charbonneau!'

'Well,' she acknowledged, 'it was worth a try. The commission would have set Tante and me up for a year.'

'Oh, I didn't mean I wouldn't buy it,' said Joel, suddenly serious. 'I think it would make a great retreat— or a conference centre, maybe. Or a home for a family with twelve children.'

Maddie's head snapped up. He was talking around the fringes of her dream, but—— 'Twelve children! Good lord!' she exclaimed.

He laughed again. 'I'll buy the thing. How much will it cost me?'

Maddie blinked. It was not Sugar Plum Fairies dancing in front of her eyes, or progressively higher sales commissions. No, it was some deep sense of loss. He wanted to fill the house with conferences. Big men with briefcases, secretaries, and bad manners. 'It'll cost a lot,' she stammered, adding another twenty thousand dollars to the total she had already arrived at. 'Three hundred and ninety thousand dollars.' The sum came out in a wistful tone. Maddie could not even *imagine* such a sum.

'Done,' Joel agreed, proffering a hand to seal the deal. She took it with exaggerated care. Joel Fairmont is a writer, and hasn't even finished his first book, her conscience screamed at her. He can't possibly afford this monstrous house! So don't worry, she told herself, stamping down the rebellion with force. Think of the commission if he *can* afford it! She stared into the fire, dreaming, until he snapped his fingers under her nose and brought her back to the present.

'So, you've listed all the things we *can't* do,' he coaxed. 'Now, what *can* we do?'

She smiled up at him. 'At first light tomorrow, we have to have a signal ready.'

'Oh? What sort?'

'There's a flagpole outside,' Maddie mused. 'We need something to fly from the flagpole. And someone to climb up the pole first thing in the morning and hang it out. The Coast Guard knows nobody lives here on the island, so that would alert them.'

'I have a vague idea who's going to be volunteered to shin up the pole,' he laughed. 'Any suggestions about what we could fly?'

'I—I don't know.' She shook her head from side to side, swinging her fast-drying brown curls around her puzzled face. 'I don't think this velvet would last in the wind. We need something that would catch the eye of a young pilot in a hurry.'

Joel chuckled as he got up. She instantly missed the warmth of him against her back. 'I suppose the pilots are mostly men?' he queried.

'I suppose so,' she said uninterestedly.

'Then we'll fly this little distress flag,' he told her, flaunting her delicate white lace teddy in her face.

She shook her head, discouraged. 'Is that all you think about?' she asked.

'What? Rescue?'

'No. I—er—oh, forget it!'

'S-E-X,' he spelled, laughing at the blush that ran up her cheeks. 'As you lectured Tante. It never goes away, does it!'

'No, I suppose not,' she said ruefully. 'But all I know about is the second-best route to a man's heart. Sit down and have some chicken, Joel. It's all that stands between us and starvation!'

CHAPTER SEVEN

THEY DINED by firelight. Joel rummaged through the pantry adjacent to the kitchen, and came up with all sorts of emergency supplies. A lantern, first aid kit, a large sleeping bag sealed in plastic, and an equally large duvet also sealed in plastic; everything a careful householder might store away for emergencies.

'Here's a little something else,' he added, and produced a dusty old wine bottle. 'A claret, 1926 vintage. It'll either be ambrosia or vinegar.'

'Where in the world did you find that?' Madeleine asked. 'You make a first-rate forager, Joel.' Her lovely face, marked by moving shadows, showed for a moment all she felt. He noted, and a small smile played across his lips as he uncorked the bottle.

'There's a sub-cellar,' he announced, holding the bottle up to the light. 'It must have been locked for years, but the wood has all rotted around the hasp. There must be—oh—two hundred bottles in there. And a corkscrew. But no glasses. You'll have to drink from the bottle. Ladies first?'

'Ambrosia or vinegar?' she quoted his own words. 'It seems to me that the gentleman is supposed to sample the vintage first.'

'Killjoy!' he laughed as he tilted the bottle to his lips and tried a small sample. And then a much larger one. 'Ambrosia, love. Our luck is in!' He handed her the bottle and his eyes challenged.

'You'd better not be fooling me,' Maddie warned him, but the sparkle in her eyes extinguished all thoughts of anger. *What does a lady do, drinking from the bottle?* She turned it until the spot where his lips had touched was directly in front of her—and then she sipped and was pleased.

Red wine might not be appropriate with chicken, but there wasn't a great deal of chicken, and there *was* plenty of wine. Maddie was not a two-fisted drinker, but she could hold her share, and for once the wine was smooth and fragrant, and not too dry. The bouquet filled her nose, almost as if the bottle had been sealed only yesterday. The twilight faded into dark night, with the storm still hanging on, rattling the windows with its thunder, splashing cold light across the landscape from time to time. Inside, warm and dry, wrapped in her velvet curtain, Maddie relaxed, until he stirred and consulted his wristwatch.

'What time is it?' she asked dreamily, hugging herself in her little cocoon.

Joel glanced at his watch again. 'It's still stopped,' he said wryly. 'But, as an old Boy Scout——'

'Emphasis on the *old*?' she asked perkily.

'None of that, now,' he remonstrated. 'It looks to be half past bedtime. If I have to be up at dawn to shin up that flagpole, I'll need my rest. You wouldn't care to wager on which one does the climbing? Flip a coin, three out of five, or something like that?'

'Not at all,' she maintained stoutly. 'It's a man's world, they tell me. You have to expect to pay the tariff.' She looked around her at the empty room with its empty bookcases and shuddered. 'I don't think I could get much sleep on this stone floor.'

'It won't be so bad,' he promised. 'This sleeping bag has an air mattress inside, and a foot-pump to inflate it.'

Maddie sat up straight, shocked by the simple statement. 'You—you don't expect me to share that thing with you, do you?' she stuttered angrily.

'Hey, it was only a suggestion,' he replied softly as he drew her briefly into his arms again. 'You're a very young twenty-seven, my dear, aren't you?'

'Not that young,' she snapped. 'I—if you were a gentleman you'd let me have the sleeping bag——'

'And what would I do?' There was a gleam in his eye, not matched by the solemn expression on his face.

'Why, you could take the duvet and go in the next room and——'

'Whoa!' laughed Joel. 'We can't even sleep in the same room?'

'No,' she whispered.

He was instantly solemn again. 'No, of course not. It wouldn't be safe, would it?'

'No, it wouldn't,' Maddie agreed. Not safe for me. I can't trust myself with you that close! There, she told herself, you've finally admitted the truth!

He was looking down at her quizzically, a half-smile on his face. 'Life doesn't seem to be too fair,' he mused. 'You get the sleeping bag and the fire, and I get the duvet and a cold room?'

'That's about it.' It was hard to be flippant, but that was the only tone that would serve. Not for a million dollars could she admit how she really felt.

'Then I think a compromise is in order.' He came to his feet, wearing the velvet curtain like a Roman toga.

'You get the fire,' he pronounced, 'but *I* get the sleeping bag.'

'But——' Protest was no use. He picked up the bag and left through the connecting door that led into the dining-room.

It was the silence that bothered Maddie the most. The little noises of Joel's breathing, his moving around. The shadows he cast in front of the fireplace. The sturdy confidence that just seeing him there provided. Maddie shivered, wrapped herself up in the duvet, and stretched out on the hearth.

It had become extremely difficult to fight the feeling she had for him. He had zoomed from hero to villain to hero again so many times in the past that she felt like a yo-yo, spinning up and down with no control over her emotions.

Her cat. He had almost killed Mehitabel. Well, his parrot had. Or was it the other way around? Joel was an author—but had yet to write a book. Nor was he exactly starving in a garret. Two cars? Two high-priced cars! No particular money worries—at least on the surface. He proposed to buy this monstrous house, almost as if his pockets were lined with thousand-dollar bills!

He played ball with the kids in the park, and yelled at *her*. Morning, noon, or night he picked on her mercilessly. And yet, when the chips were down, he was a gentle efficient man, who knew how to handle adversity. What did she really think about him?

'Well,' she muttered, 'he built that darn fence, didn't he? Tante Marie thinks he's great. I'm beginning to think I do too! Oh, God, why does life have to be so confusing?'

She ducked her head under the duvet, a childhood habit she had never outgrown. *What I can't see, can't see me!* Joel Fairmont, mystery. With her eyes closed his head was silhouetted against the inside of her eyelids. Tall, tanned, blond hair, blue eyes, smiling that quirky little smile that teased the right side of his mouth higher than the left. Something about him has changed on this trip, she thought. It's almost as if he had some hidden motive—some plan at work. But what? Before she could reason it all out exhaustion claimed her, and she fell asleep.

Scientists say that dreams last only seconds. Maddie dreamed, disputing the figures. Her dream went on and on, as if a video tape had been spliced in a circle and replayed itself for the entire night.

Joel's head was the major part of the illusion. He was in the sleeping bag, and she was lying on top of him. She could see only his head, but could feel the contact with his warm flesh. And yet as those deep eyes sparkled at her a thousand wildly exciting impulses went dancing up and down her spine. He touched her everywhere, lightly, persuasively. When both his hands appeared to cup her face, she could still feel him touching her in more erogenous zones. She moaned and writhed, but no matter what she did at one particular point the sensations would halt, his head would disappear, and she could see, instead, the grey-white figure of Mehitabel, her cat.

The wise old feline sat primly on the floor, in some sort of circle of light, and licked his front paws. And then his head would turn in her direction and the cat would say, 'So you really want to know how to get a litter of white kittens?' And then another sudden discontinuity, and Joel's face would reappear, and the circular tape would run again.

Madeleine was almost exhausted from frustration when the tape shifted into a new sequence. A short rotund figure was outside the window, tapping. Without looking she knew it was Hiram Murchison, and him dead these many years. Tapping at the window from the outside, scrabbling against the shutters as the orchestra of Hell beat kettledrums behind him.

It couldn't be, of course. College graduates don't believe in ghosts. Haunting is for simpler minds! Maddie tried desperately to put down the panic that seized her, and ducked her head farther under the corner of the duvet. Her teeth were chattering in time with the tapping at the window. Faster, perhaps.

Again and again, the tapping at the window, and then, suddenly, a tremendous crash as whatever it was outside on the ledge came through the window. A swirl of wind roared in after him, shaking the walls, pelting the floor with huge raindrops.

Maddie was already half-way across the room before she woke up, screaming her lungs out. The interconnecting door delayed her momentarily. It swung inward, and no amount of pushing was going to force it open. Somehow a glimmer of sense broke through her panic. She seized the knob and pulled, then bolted through the opening, shaking like a leaf.

There was only one refuge. Joel was sitting up drowsily in the sleeping bag, barely aware of what was going on. She hardly waited for explanations. A head-first dive landed her on top of him, head tucked against his shoulder, screaming all the while. The screaming fell to a whimper as she struggled to get closer to him. He lay back in the bed for a second, until his mind shifted gears, and then he enveloped her naked body with his warm arms, and struggled to unzip the bag and take her inside. And all the while he whispered comforting noises at her ear. Not exactly words, just noises.

Gradually, as the warmth surrounded her, she sensed his protective presence. The shivering slowed, and eventually stopped. The tears, which total fright had forbidden, began to come, like little quiet rivulets down her cheeks, splashing off his nude chest.

'Cry it out,' he coaxed softly. 'Cry it out.' His arms tightened around her back. It all had a dreamlike quality, Maddie thought, her first sensible thought in all this night. There's his head, here we are touching at all points, north and south, only I'm on top. The logic of it stifled the tears. She sniffed a couple of times and raised her head.

'I—I'm sorry,' she stammered. Joel smiled up at her.

'No need to apologise,' he comforted. 'I was scared half to death when I heard the noise.'

She searched out each little cranny of his mobile face, and gently pushed his vagrant lock of hair back. 'You never were,' she stated lovingly. 'I know better. Nothing frightens you.'

'A lot you know,' chuckled Joel. '*You* scare me. Shall we go take a look?'

The casualness of it brought Maddie back to reality. Here she was, totally naked, sharing a bed with a man in the same condition, and crying all over his chest. *I* scare him? Not likely, she thought, as she rolled off him on to her side. She might have rolled out of the bag entirely, but his arms still held her. At least that was the excuse she used. The truth was much too simple. She didn't *want* to escape him. Nor did she want to set foot in that other room again—not tonight! 'I—don't think I can,' she murmured. 'It was Hiram Murchison!'

'Climbing through the window?' he chuckled. 'You're a victim of your own superstitions, Maddie Charbonneau.' He treasured her body with one more gentle hug. 'We've got to do something about that name of yours. Charbonneau. It takes too much effort to spell it.' He patted the back of her head, and cautiously kissed the tip of her nose. 'And now I think I'd better go see what happened.'

'No—I——' She curled up into a ball as he withdrew his arms, already missing the warmth, the comfort of him. He slid off the edge of the bed and fumbled for a moment in the darkness. The light, when it came, flickered and then settled as the lantern sputtered. The weak yellow glow splashed shadows across his body. Maddie stared, fascinated. He was the first virile male she had ever seen completely naked. The light played games with the massive muscles of his shoulders, high-lighted the tiny curls on his chest. The light blond scattering was arranged in the shape of a T, the bar extending across between his nipples, the stem leading down into the shadows of his abdomen. Maddie licked her lips nervously, but could not give up the looking. When he moved the lantern ahead of him, she almost cried at the loss.

'Now what?' asked Joel from out of the darkness.

'Nothing,' she gasped. 'Just—be careful. There's glass on the floor in there.' Then he and the light were gone. Maddie closed her eyes and scuttled deeper into the bed, until the sheet covered her head. And waited.

He was back sooner than she had expected. She heard the hissing of the lantern as he turned it off. The other side of the air mattress sank under his weight. And still she hid.

His body was cold when it pressed up against hers. Her head bobbed as his arm slipped under her neck and drew her over to him. 'It's all over,' he said softly, pulling the sheet down to uncover her head. 'Old Hiram has gone.'

'What—was it?' she asked nervously. Not from ghostly fears, but rather purely physical ones. His hand had come all the way around, and rested just below her right breast. The thought of it, poised there, waiting, excited her. And frightened her. She squirmed an extra inch or two away from him, and his grip tightened.

'The big oak tree alongside the house,' he reported casually. 'The storm finally got to it, and it came down on the house. I imagine there's some roof damage. One of the branches came through the window at you. Satisfied?'

'Oh.' A deflated comment. It was much more believable that Hiram Murchison was out there, seeking vengeance on *somebody*! 'Then I guess I could go back.' Almost a whisper, that, and a prayer.

'If you want to.' His hands moved not an inch. His voice was as casual as if they were sharing Tante Marie's tea in the kitchen on McGrath Street. Maddie moved one foot tentatively out, and instantly brought it back.

'I—don't want to,' she sighed, shifting against him. That waiting hand moved, climbed the mountain of desire, and poised at its bronze peak. Instantly she was wide awake, listening to her own pulse hammer as blood coursed madly through her veins. She squeezed her eyes tightly closed, shivering. Mehitabel appeared inside her eyelids, and that strange voice whispered 'kittens?'. It was enough of a shock. Madeleine's hands locked on his, moving it back to the safety of her flat stomach. It moved without objection.

'I—don't want that,' she lied. 'I—I'm tired, and—just totally beat. I hope——'

'Then go to sleep,' Joel said softly, and the deep rumble of his voice bathed her in comfort again. She shifted her weight a couple of times, then, almost drowsily, moved until her head rested on his chest before she dropped off. He cuddled her head against him, careful not to trespass. And so Maddie slept through the long night while Joel lay there, rigidly fighting his own demons. The storm broke about two o'clock in the morning, and in the sudden quiet even he slept. And kept his dreams to himself.

'Maddie? Maddie!' Someone was shaking her shoulder and she didn't want to wake up. Some hard hand, not Tante Marie's soft touch. She managed to get one eyelid to open. Joel was bent over her bed, dressed in slacks and shirt and smile, and light was pouring in through the window.

Maddie groped for a moment, remembering, then sat up with a little squeak of alarm, clutching the cover to her breasts.

'Now, none of that,' he said cheerfully. 'The airplane has come for us. Up you get. I've brought your clothes. Everything's in good shape—except for your—whatever you call that thing you wore underneath. I'm afraid that's stuck up on the flagpole.'

'The airplane?' stuttered Maddie.

'Has come for us,' he laughed, completing the sentence. 'He must have seen the flag. He circled the island a couple of times, landed out in the channel, and came ashore in a little rubber boat. Can you get ready?'

'Yes,' she croaked, then cleared her throat and tried again. 'If you'll—step outside while I dress.'

'Why, you're blushing,' he observed. 'You don't see much of that these days!'

'Maybe not in your society,' she snapped, and was instantly contrite. 'I'm sorry. You were so good to me—during our shipwreck. And imagine, Hiram Murchison! That's a story I can tell my customers next fall.'

'All of it?' he teased, and laughed again as she turned blush-red in every conceivable place.

'Get out of here, you—you roué,' she laughed. Joel went, but not before he dropped a kiss on the tip of her nose. Maddie sat up and watched as the door closed behind him, then gently rubbed the spot which his lips had anointed.

'I won't wash that spot for a month,' she told herself jokingly. The little voice of her conscience, deep in her head, commented, *What a good idea!* Surprised and embarrassed, she slid out of bed and dressed with all due haste.

Joel was outside in the sunshine when Maddie came down the veranda stairs, balancing carefully in her boots. The little cut on her foot bothered her slightly, but she had no intention of collecting another slice by going barefoot. Joel was talking with an older man, who wore the inevitable flight jacket of the local Lake pilots.

'Jimmy Murphy,' Joel introduced. 'Our rescue crew.'

'You don't work for the Coast Guard,' Maddie commented. 'I know all those people. But we're thankful that you came by, anyhow.'

She wanted to say something else, but Joel interrupted with a briskness that wasn't normal to him. 'Let's get going,' he said as he took her arm. 'The sooner we get back to Laconia the sooner we can explain all this to your aunt.'

'That makes sense,' Maddie agreed, and the three of them went off down the path.

'Slippery along here,' warned Murphy as they came to the first change of direction. Maddie felt Joel's grip tighten on her forearm, and put her own hand on top of his as a sign of—well, approval. A flutter in the tall grass near his foot startled Joel.

'What the hell?' he muttered as he pulled Maddie to a stop. Two little quails ran across the path in front of them, and disappeared into the bush on the other side.

'Bob Whites,' she said. 'There are all sorts of birds out here. Nobody ever comes.' She gestured off to their right, where they could hear the clatter of a red-headed woodpecker at work.

'And don't forget the gulls,' added Murphy. 'I knew there was a storm coming yesterday. All the gulls came ashore, and roosted on the flat roof of the supermarket.'

'I suppose your—guests at your conference centre will want to shoot them all, Joel,' Maddie suggested sadly.

'They hadn't better,' he threatened. 'We'll post the island as a bird sanctuary.' Maddie took a deep breath and smiled at him. One more good mark on his side of the ledger.

'You must have been surprised to see our distress flag, Mr Murphy,' she called to the pilot, who was out ahead of them.

'Oh, I was,' he answered, looking back over his shoulder. 'I never did——'

'It isn't important,' Joel interrupted. 'What we need is a quick trip back to the metropolis.' Maddie, busy observing the bright green world, and measuring the aftermath of the storm, missed the look that flashed between the two men.

The rubber boat was aground on the tiny beach where the wharf had been the night before. Nothing was left of that structure except for one bollard, standing alone in about five feet of water. There was nothing to be seen of Henri's runabout.

'Oh dear,' she sighed as she climbed into the boat, shedding her shoes to avoid puncturing its bottom with her stiletto heels. 'How am I going to explain all this to Henri?'

'It doesn't need an explanation,' Joel returned gruffly. 'The boat was lost due to an Act of God. Or you can charge it off to the sale of the estate if you want to.'

In her excitement, Maddie had almost forgotten that. The sale of the Murchison estate! There was no doubt that Henri could buy himself a *couple* of new boats with that commission! And why is it that every time I mention Henri, Joel goes all gruff and snarling? she wondered.

'Then you haven't changed your mind?' she asked wistfully, and immediately wished she hadn't.

'No, I haven't changed my mind,' he said solemnly. 'It'll make a great conference centre.'

'But why in the world would a writer want a conference centre?'

'Maddie,' he grumbled, 'I'm tired. I didn't get much sleep last night. Or the night before, for that matter. Why don't you do me a big favour and shut up?'

'Well, *that's* not very nice,' she muttered. But she *did* shut up, turning her attention to the voyage as the little battery-operated outboard motor pushed their clumsy little craft out to where the aircraft lay at anchor.

The Lake was like a millpond, with not enough breeze to lift Maddie's uncombed hair. She used her fingers to effect some repair, but there was not much to be done about her blouse. Dry it was, but wrinkled, and the two top buttons were missing. Joel had never returned her hairpins, the ones he had used to pick the lock the previous night.

She had a little trouble transferring from the bobbing rubber boat on to the Cessna's pontoon, and then up into the cabin. Once inside she sought the back seat behind the pilot, and felt a little stab when Joel elected to sit up front. But that, she told herself, is the way men are. They always want to sit up front, to be in control— and the sooner I learn how to handle that, the better off I'll be. So she rested her head against the coolness of the rear window, and fell asleep again, missing completely the short, quiet flight over the beautiful world, and their landing on the seastrip off Christmas Island.

It was the silence that awakened her. The big motor ceased to roar, and the plane glided smoothly to an anchorage. Joel helped her out of the cabin, down to the waiting job boat, and out on to the wooden dock under the brow of Weirs Boulevard. He was being so solicitous that she almost missed the fact that his LeBaron convertible, the car they had left in the car park at Weirs Beach, was waiting for them. A small suspicion jumped to the front of her mind, and she asked him about it.

'Nothing miraculous,' he reported as he handed her into the car. 'Haven't you heard of radio? I asked Murphy to have it picked up and brought over here. Now can we go?'

Maddie offered him her best smile and leaned back in the seat as the powerful engine began the work of taking them home. Laconia had never looked so good. Everything from streets to buildings was surrounded by a pleasant haze. All in her mind, she knew, but pleasant none the less. And when they turned in under the shade of the maple trees that lined McGrath Street she felt a nagging urge to run up to the house, slam all the doors, and tell Tante Marie what a wonderful day it was.

Joel gave her a head start, remaining in the car and laughing as her tall graceful figure disappeared. He could hear her calling inside, then silence. He gave her about five more minutes by the clock on his dashboard, then climbed out of the car and went up to the door.

Maddie was standing in the kitchen, a dazed expression on her face. Bluebeard, locked inside his cage on top of the refrigerator, was muttering, 'Pretty baby,' over and over again. Mehitabel sat outside the screen door on the veranda, and scratched as soon as he heard Maddie's voice.

'What's the trouble?' asked Joel as he came over to her and put a welcome arm around her shoulder.

'I don't know,' she whispered. 'Tante Marie isn't here!'

'That's nothing to worry about,' he assured her. 'She might have gone out with some of her friends. She might even be up at my house. My mother was due in yesterday, you know.'

'No,' she snapped stubbornly. 'Tante would have left me a note. She'd be worried enough because I didn't get home last night. No, she wouldn't have gone off——'

She ducked under his arm and ran for the living room. By the time he caught up she was dialling the telephone. 'Police,' she said, 'I want to talk to the chief.' There was a moment of silence while she listened. 'No,' she said firmly, 'I don't want to talk to the desk sergeant. I want to talk to Uncle Fred—the chief. Yes, my Uncle Fred!'

She covered the mouthpiece with one hand as she waited. 'They don't like people who call asking for the chief,' she told him. 'I hate to pull rank, but——'

'But what are uncles for?' Joel finished the statement.

And then someone said something at the other end of the telephone, and Maddie muttered, 'Oh, my God,' as she gently returned the instrument to its cradle.

'What is it?' he asked softly, holding out both hands to her. She took them, her own hands suddenly chilled.

'Uncle Fred's at the hospital,' she said, and he could hear all the misery in the world in her voice. 'They admitted Tante Marie this morning!'

CHAPTER EIGHT

'I CALLED the hospital,' Maddie explained as she hurried down the stairs. 'They said Tante was doing as well as can be expected, and I couldn't see her before twelve o'clock this morning.' She brushed at her neat grey suit and rearranged the lace down the front of her white blouse. 'I—don't trust hospitals when they talk like that, but Tante would be embarrassed if I didn't wear a dress, and——'

'Hey, don't let it worry you,' said Joel in that hearty sort of voice that people use when they are saying what they think you want to hear. 'I'm sure it means just what they said.'

Maddie's head snapped up. His forehead was wrinkled with concern, and she didn't like the look in his eyes. Strange thoughts rattled around in her head—Tante is in her eighties. She stared at him, pleading wordlessly for assurance, and received none. 'Let's hurry!' she cried.

'Relax, Madeleine.' His big hand dropped on her shoulder and wheeled her around in front of the wall mirror. 'We have an hour before she can see us. Relax.' Her hands went unconsciously to her hair, pushing back a curl here and there as she bit her lip in frustration. The soft, silken hair was not about to be disciplined. Maddie gave it up as a bad job, and managed with an unsteady hand to add a little neutral gloss to her lips.

'How far are we from the hospital?' asked Joel.

'About ten minutes,' she said. 'Do I look all right?'

'Of course you do,' he assured her.

And so do you, she thought. He had gone up to his own house and changed into a three-piece grey suit and a tie. His suit was almost a match for hers. His blond hair was combed back and glistened—water perhaps. Unconsciously her fingers probed and confirmed. He caught her hand as she withdrew, and kissed the open palm before releasing her. Those deep blue eyes sparkled pleasure at her. The square strong face wrinkled with a smile that was like a welcome home. He towered satisfactorily over her. Wanting the contrast, urgently needing it, Maddie had slipped into a pair of flatties.

'OK, then we'd better get going,' he said solemnly. There, she told herself angrily, he knew what I was doing, and he's pitying me! Her temper flared and then was instantly quashed. What's the use? she teased herself wryly. You fell in love with him at first sight; so what else is new? He doesn't love you, and there's nothing much you can do about it, is there? Your little plot to get him to move away has only made things worse. At least before you *doubted* what a fool you are, and now you're sure!

Joel's hand cupped her elbow comfortably as he escorted her out to the car. Back to the Mustang this time, she noted. He caught her expression. 'We don't want your hair blowing all over the place,' he explained as he handed her into her seat.

Maddie's fears for Tante Marie overwhelmed every other thought, and she hardly noticed as he found his way over to Union Avenue, then turned right and cruised on down to Elliot Street without asking for directions.

The Lakes Region General Hospital was perhaps not the largest hospital in the world, but it had a steady inflow of customers—half-drowned and sunburned tourists in the summer, and an overflow of broken legs from the ski-lodges in the winter. Tante Marie was segregated in a small double room at the very back of the establishment. The other bed was empty.

Maddie hurried into the room, ignoring the woman at the nursing station. Tante Marie lay squarely in the middle of the big hospital bed, whose head had been elevated to a semi-sitting position. She looked like a frail little doll in her old-fashioned lace-trimmed nightgown, her hair meticulously brushed. Both her hands were outside the sheets, lying parallel to her stick-figure body. Uncle Fred heaved his bulky form up from the chair by the bed as Madeleine and Joel came in.

'Well, Maddie's here. I think it's a good idea you checked into the hospital,' he growled as he swept by them, dropping a kiss on Madeleine's forehead. 'It's about time you took care of yourself!'

'That's the police chief?' Joel queried as the older man walked by them out into the corridor.

'No, that's Uncle Fred,' Maddie half-whispered. 'He's much more diplomatic when he's wearing his police hat!' They both turned towards the bed. Tante Marie looked so tiny, bundled under the sheets, with a terribly tired expression on her face.

'Oh, Tante!' Maddie cried as she hurried across the room and knelt at the side of the bed. One thin old hand came up and rested gently on the top of her head.

'What's the matter, child?' Tante Marie lifted herself upward on one elbow. Joel hastily moved to the foot of the bed and found the crank to elevate it a little higher. The old lady smiled her thanks, and relaxed.

'It was the storm,' Maddie murmured. 'We were at Glory Island and the storm came up. So we went up to the Murchison manor for shelter—and the boat was wrecked. So we—had to spend the night. I feel terrible for having worried you so much!'

Tante smiled gently. 'I wasn't worried,' she said gently. 'Joel left a note saying you would be spending the night with friends. The only thing that bothers me is that I'm afraid of hospitals. You know what a coward I am. They've been poking and prying at me for ages. But now I really feel well, seeing you both happily together!'

'Oh, Tante!' gasped Madeleine. Joel moved up behind her and put a comforting hand on her shoulder.

'No, I wasn't really *terribly* worried,' the frail old lady continued, considerably more cheerfully. 'I knew Joel was with you—and I have boundless confidence in him. Who were the friends you stayed with?'

'Friends?' Maddie stammered. 'We——'

'We were alone,' Joel interrupted. 'Just the two of us.'

'Just the two of you?' Those sharp old eyes searched them both, and the little smile faded slightly.

Joel stepped in at that point and told the entire story, every excruciating moment, paying no attention to Maddie's half-hidden protests.

By the time his tale came to an end, Tante Marie looked more bewildered than shocked. 'Your niece did nothing she ought to be ashamed of,' he added.

'I don't remember anybody saying anything about shame,' the old lady stated firmly. 'I've never been ashamed of my niece, and I don't expect to start now. Stop crying, Madeleine! There's my girl.' The mottled old hand patted Maddie's head gently, ruffling through her lush brown hair as it had done in her childhood.

'I'm so happy you understand, Tante.' Maddie smiled for the first time since the interrogation had begun. 'I suppose there are many in Laconia who wouldn't.'

'Of course,' the old lady mused, 'times have changed greatly since I was a girl, love. The telephone, the radio, the television, cars, women working outside the home. Everything changes—but not human nature. But then we needn't worry, love. The neighbours will gossip. I don't have enough years left in me to worry, and you're young enough to be able to go someplace else if you have to. Don't worry about it at all. Mr Fairmont is a nice man. The whole town will know about it by nightfall, but there's no need for us to be concerned about town gossip!' She fell back against her pillow, smiling, her worn eyes sparking with some inner light.

There was colour in the old lady's cheeks too. Almost as if she were happy about something, Madeleine told herself. 'Oh, Tante,' she murmured, the words barely breasting the tears, 'I'd do anything—anything to help you get better.'

'I don't think there's anything that would help,' the old lady sighed, speaking slowly as if the weight of all her years lay over every syllable. 'But my greatest wish has always been that——'

'I think I have the answer,' Joel interrupted. 'Madeleine and I will get married. Won't that solve the problem?'

The words hit Maddie's mind like a nuclear bomb going off. *Madeleine and I will get married!* Of all the improbable gifts on her Christmas tree, there was nothing she wanted more than that! Nothing! And still——

'You can't do that,' she protested. 'I couldn't *ask* you to do that! My reputation isn't that important!'

'You don't have to ask me,' he assured her. 'I'm asking you. And your reputation and your aunt's *are* that important. Furthermore, since I'm the cause of the problem, I should be the *solution* to the problem.'

'I've always wanted to see you married,' the old lady admitted. 'It would be a wonderful thing, Madeleine, if you could see your way clear, not because of this silly gossip thing, but because you—well, you know. You need a strong man, my dear. Marriage to a weak one would ruin you. But with a man like Joel—it would be wonderful.'

Maddie searched her aunt's face. The old woman was all smiles, a gleam in her eye, more colour to her cheeks, an eagerness the girl had not seen in years.

'I'd be happy to marry you, Madeleine,' Joel repeated as he moved closer and put an arm around her shoulders.

'For Tante's sake?' she muttered, half in protest.

'For all our sakes,' he insisted.

Maddie glowed all over as she turned back to her aunt. 'There, Tante, it's settled. Now you get better quickly so you can come to the wedding.'

'I need to speak to my girl,' Joel announced. He took Maddie's arm and towed her out of the room into the hall.

'You don't have to play Tarzan,' she snapped at him, rubbing her arm. 'I'll have a bruise for sure!'

'Don't worry about a little thing like bruises,' he hissed at her. 'Can't you see the gleam in your aunt's eyes? The flushed cheeks? She's sick, Madeleine. That's a sign of fever. She has to avoid morbid excitement! She wants very much to see you get married, and if you put it off until tomorrow—who knows if there'll be a tomorrow!'

'Oh, my!' Madeleine sagged against him as her knees lost their strength. That hovering fear was back again. 'She's dying?'

'I don't know,' Joel replied. 'I'm not a doctor. But are you sure she *isn't*? Are you willing to take that chance?'

'No,' she replied, 'I—I don't want to do that. But how——?'

'We get married right here, and right now,' he said firmly. 'At Tante's bedside. I just happened to see the hospital chaplain a couple of doors down as we came in. I'm sure I can get his agreement.'

'But—but we need a licence, and that takes time,' she objected.

He waved the argument aside. 'Let me take care of the details, Maddie.'

They went back into the sickroom, arm in arm. 'Tante!' Maddie called. The old lady opened her eyes.

'I wasn't sleeping,' she insisted. 'Just resting my eyes. They poked and prodded me so much today I feel as if I've been in an accident. Now, what have you been up to? Setting the wedding date?'

'Exactly,' Joel grinned down at her. 'Would you mind being our witness?'

'I don't know when I can.' Tante waved a vague hand at the hospital area around her.

'Not to worry,' he assured her. 'If you can stand the shock, we're going to be married right here by your bed.'

'Oh, my!' Tante struggled to sit up again. 'When do you plan to *have* this ceremony?'

'In about ten minutes,' he offered. 'If you approve of your niece marrying me?'

'Ten minutes?' she gasped. 'Of course I approve! Maddie?'

'Ten minutes?' gasped Maddie, fingering her blouse.

'Ten minutes,' Joel said firmly. 'You two smile at each other, and I'll go down the hall and see about the chaplain.' He leaned down and gave each of them a kiss on the cheek. Before Maddie could object he was gone.

'Hold my hand,' her aunt said, almost chortling in her happiness. Maddie complied.

The door behind her opened and closed. Madeleine smiled over her shoulder at Joel—but it was Henri instead, his shining pate wet with perspiration. Joel was a few steps behind him.

'I came as soon as I could,' Henri said excitedly. 'But the message was garbled. What is it, Madeleine?'

'So you're Henri,' Joel said coldly as he came back into the room behind the estate agent. The short, rotund man stared up at the tall slim one, and instant antagonism flashed between them.

'I don't know about the message,' Maddie stammered. 'Was it about my wedding?'

'Ah, at last!' Henri shouted. His feet managed to turn his bulk around in a dancing circle. 'So you finally came to your senses, Madeleine!'

'Yes, I guess I did,' she responded hesitantly. 'But——'

'But it's just the right time.' Henri sounded like a man who had just won the New England lottery. 'The Realtors' Convention opens in Albany the day after tomorrow. We can take our honeymoon and attend the convention all at the same time.'

'Oh, Henri!' sighed Maddie. Her aunt opened her eyes and glanced at them, then retreated behind her eyelids again.

'I think you've got the wrong script,' Joel interrupted, his deep heavy voice overriding whatever it was that Henri was trying to say. '*I'm* the bridegroom, not you!'

Henri looked stricken. His usually red face paled, and he grabbed a handkerchief from his coat pocket and wiped his forehead with it. 'Maddie? You can't do this to me,' he pleaded. 'You break my heart!'

'Tell him about the sale of the Murchison place,' Joel commanded, looking and acting his most arrogant.

The little man drew himself up to his full five feet four and glared back. 'You think a mere house sale could repair a broken heart?'

'And I smashed your boat, too,' she confessed dolefully. 'It broke up in the storm. There isn't a single piece left.'

'Tell him about the sale price on the house. I'm sure he has boat insurance,' Joel commanded. His head nodded to reinforce the command, and his fierce eyes left her no escape. She leaned over and whispered in Henri's ear.

The estate agent's eyes widened as he listened. 'You're sure?'

'I'm sure,' said Joel. 'Stay for the wedding. You could be a witness.'

The little man considered for a moment. 'Well, money doesn't cure a broken heart,' he sighed, 'but a great deal of it can soothe the pain.'

'Then you should be feeling pure bliss,' Joel muttered.

Madeleine stared at the pair of them. Henri she could understand—he was a man who loved deeply and sincerely; his wallet was the target of all that affection. Joel left her completely confused. If she didn't know better, she would swear he was exhibiting signs of terminal jealousy. She was about to spear him with a question when two more people came into the room. The first one she knew—the Reverend Harry LeDeux. The other was a woman of about fifty, tall, gaunt, wearing the mark of a thousand crusades on her face.

'Oh, hell,' Joel said flatly. 'What are *you* doing here, Mother?'

'I think everything is in order,' Reverend LeDeux announced. He rubbed his hands together in great glee. 'This is exciting, isn't it? I've never done one exactly like this! Is this the little bride?'

Maddie had never felt less like being a *little* bride. Save for Joel, she towered over everyone in the room. The good Reverend hardly topped five foot six, and his thin frame was slightly bent in the middle. She gave him a hesitant nod.

'Exciting,' the Reverend repeated as he turned towards Tante Marie. 'And this is the mother of the bride?' Tante almost strangled in her bed, so eager was she to correct him, but he had passed on like the wind before she managed a word. 'And you are——' he said cheerfully, turning to Joel's mother.

'What's going on here!' Mrs Fairmont's roar sounded exactly like the opening gun of World War Three.

'That's my mother,' Joel interjected. 'She's not necessary to the occasion. I'm getting married, Mother.'

Mrs Fairmont glared at her son and then at Madeleine. 'The child really doesn't know what she's getting into!

What a fool you are, Joel. Flesh of my flesh, and a fool. I'll tell her myself!'

'One of your major faults, Mother, is that you talk too much. I think I might have put up with things if you'd ever learned to keep your mouth shut!'

'Joel!' Madeleine was scandalised by the conversation. In her mountain life nobody talked to their mother *that* way!

He gave Maddie one quick look. 'Shut up, Maddie,' he ordered, then returned his attention to the other woman. 'One more word, Mother, and your allowance cheque won't come next month!' He spat the words out like bullets from a machine gun, and his mother swallowed the rest of what she wanted to say and choked on the mess.

'Start the ceremony,' said Tante in a surprisingly strong voice. She was instantly the centre of attention. 'I don't—have a great deal of time to waste. I need my rest.'

Dr Burton, who had just come in at the rear of the crowd, seemed to have caught a bad cold. His cough choked him. Reverend LeDeux mustered bride and groom on the same side of the bed, went to the other side himself, and towed Henri along with him. Mrs Fairmont snapped her mouth shut and stood grimly at the foot of the bed, looking as if she were invoking gypsy curses on the lot of them.

'Now then,' the good reverend said as he opened his prayer book. 'Dearly beloved——'

Madeleine stood rigidly beside her bridegroom, unable to turn her head far enough to the right to see him. His hand held hers loosely. Tante Marie stared at her with a terrible intensity, all her love in her eyes.

Words tumbled around Maddie's ears but not into them. She might well have been alone, rather than the centre of such a mixed crowd. Standing alone, concentrating. Let it be done and over before Tante—she muttered to herself. Let her feel the joy of it, if that's what she wants. As I would if I thought this man beside me had any affection for me. Why is he doing all this?

He jerked her hand once, and then again. She lifted her head. The chaplain was staring at her expectantly. Joel leaned over and whispered, 'Say, I will.'

'I will,' she managed to get out. Immediately the service moved into high gear again, and left her swamped and somewhat bereft. It wasn't at all what she had dreamed.

Those long youthful summer dreams, in which Madeleine Charbonneau walked down the aisle in her long white dress to the bridal processional march, and a tall man without a face awaited her at the altar. All gone. There were flowers—a bouquet beside Tante's bed. But the scent of the flowers could not compete with the smell of antiseptics. And this is the seal that's to last all my life, she told herself ruefully. But perhaps he intends it to be only for Tante's last few hours?

Tante's pale eyes showed a little wet. The old lady was crying, and trying not to. The room was silent, as if the world had turned off every noise. The silence hung in a cloud over the bed, and over the participants.

'—pronounce you man and wife,' the Reverend LeDeux said happily. 'You may kiss the bride.'

Maddie was still rigidly fixed in position, her hands folded in front of her. Joel turned her slowly in his direction and kissed her gently on the cheek.

'I won't put up with this,' Mrs Fairmont threatened as she made for the door. 'We have a great deal to talk about, Joel!'

'The witness should sign here,' the chaplain said.

'Thank God it's over.' Tante was hoarse, but still audible.

'About that sale?' Henri asked eagerly as he signed his name three times, once in the wrong place.

'I'll be in touch,' said Joel. 'For God's sake, man, this is a wedding, not a convention.'

Maddie broke out of her daze and knelt at the bedside again while the men fiddled about with papers and certificates, and who knew what else. 'Tante? You're all right? It's done. I hope it made you happy.'

Her great-aunt opened one eye and managed a bright smile. 'Yes, child, it's done and I'm happy—as you will be. He's a good man. Trust him.'

'I—yes, of course,' Maddie stammered. 'I—yes.'

'All right, everybody,' Dr Burton announced, 'the limit is two visitors per patient, and you're all half an hour past visiting hours. Clear out!'

'Come along, Maddie,' her new husband said softly. 'Let me take you home.'

'My congratulations,' the Reverend LeDeux repeated as he shook the hand of both bride and groom and hurried out of the door.

'Like the White Rabbit in *Alice in Wonderland*,' murmured Joel as they watched the man go.

'I'll be in touch on the details of the Murchison house,' Henri bubbled as he passed them by. 'Oh, I almost forgot—congratulations!'

'Yeah,' Joel said as he ushered Maddie out into the hall. 'Congratulations to us all. Let's go home, wife.'

Inside the room Dr Burton checked to see that all had gone before he turned back to the bed. 'I don't really understand what's going on,' he announced, shaking his head. 'You come into the hospital for your annual physical, and your great-niece seems to have come unglued.'

'Don't ask me what it's all about,' Tante Marie said stoutly. 'Maddie was the one who insisted, and set up all the appointments three months ago. You'll have to finish quickly. I can't help having the feeling that there are going to be exciting things happen in my house. And I look forward to them eagerly!'

'No more excitement,' the doctor insisted. 'I'll tell your new son-in-law. He looks as if he might be able to take you in hand—the pair of you, for that matter. What's his name?'

'Fairmont,' sighed Tante. 'Isn't that a romantic name?'

'Robideaux would have been better,' the doctor laughed as he tucked the disc of his stethoscope back into his pocket and wandered out of the door.

Maddie maintained her silence all the way out to the car. When Joel came around and joined her inside she managed a weak smile. 'She *seemed* to be happy.'

'She was. Be assured, Madeleine, she was. It was a wonderful thing you did.' Joel turned the key, and the little Mustang powered into action and pulled them out of the car park and back on to Elliot Street.

'It was a wonderful thing *you* did,' Maddie murmured. 'I don't know how to thank you, Joel. It was all so surprising. I had no idea—well, I knew Tante

wanted to see me married, but I hadn't expected anything so sudden. Am I making sense?'

'Of course you are. You always do. You're a very level-
headed lady, Madeleine Fairmont.' He took one hand
off the wheel and reached over to pat her knee.

'I don't feel like one right now. My world is still going
around in circles.' She fell silent, making no protest about
his hand, which was still on her knee. It felt right. She
was Mrs Fairmont. Mrs Madeleine Fairmont. Enjoy it
while you can, Maddie, she told herself.

Joel motored into the driveway of her house and
turned off the engine. A pair of slit eyes glared at them
from the front porch. Mehitabel was standing guard.
From somewhere up on the second floor Bluebeard was
screaming away at the top of his lungs. 'Crazy cat!' the
bird squawked. 'Man the lifeboats. Pretty baby.'

'Well, at least they're still alive,' Maddie said ruefully.
'Won't you come in for a cup of coffee?'

Joel looked at her peculiarly. 'I do believe I will.'

She slipped out of the car and walked gracefully up
to the front door, swaying slightly as she went. He
watched, grinning. It *had* gone well, he acknowledged,
as he climbed out of the car and picked up his luggage
from the boot. But that was only the first act. The second
might be more difficult.

'I only hope my mother is up here just for the day,'
he muttered as he followed Maddie into the house. There
was a slight uproar as Mehitabel and Bluebeard both
extended congratulations and were fed. And then they
seemed to gravitate to the kitchen, and coffee.

Look at him, Maddie thought, staring across the table.
Big and capable and warm, and all mine! Her heart ex-
panded far enough to put a strain on her chest. But there

was something eating at her. She concentrated, trying to marshal all the little clues that had dropped during the day. 'Joel, I think you and I need to have a little talk.'

'OK,' he replied. 'Fire away.'

'There's something funny going on around here, Joel Fairmont. Probably several somethings. But I can only handle one at a time.'

He brushed the lock of hair out of his eyes and smiled at her as he pulled his chair closer to hers.

'I have this feeling. Well, it's more than a feeling. You are definitely *not* a writer!'

'That's not quite true,' he defended. 'I'm *almost* a writer. I want to *be* a writer. But there's this family business hanging over my head. It feeds and clothes my mother and me and a host of relatives. I've been neglecting it—if that's the right word. I never *wanted* to be in the business. I always said that. I hated it, until you said something to me on our way to Weirs Beach the other day. Do you remember?'

'I'm afraid not,' she mused. 'That seems to be ten years ago—all of that.'

'You said that it didn't matter what you did, as long as you did it to the best of your ability. Remember? And that set me to thinking. I've been playing at living, avoiding all my responsibilities, and you set me right with one quick word, lady. So now, no more embarrassment. I'm going to be the best in New England, the finest——'

'Grocery clerk!' she squealed in amazement. 'Fairmont! Fairways! Fairways Supermarkets?'

'I knew you were too smart to be fooled for ever,' he laughed. 'Fairways Supermarkets. Fifty-two stores throughout New England! I'm the chief operating of-

ficer, and you're my vice-president in charge of everything else.'

'Hey,' she protested, 'what do I know——'

'You know what you want from a supermarket,' he
said, leaning over the table to catch her hand. 'And I
know what I want from you. We'll make a wonderful
team, Madeleine, at home and away!'

'Why, Joel Fairmont,' she sighed happily as she stood
up, 'I thought you were a sheep in sheep's clothing, and
instead you're a—drink your coffee while it's still hot!'

CHAPTER NINE

'THEY'VE all gone?' Maddie dropped on to the sofa in the living-room and put her feet up on Tante's footstool. The late evening sun was barely visible over the mountain tops that surrounded the city. *I've been a married woman for twelve hours!* The thought hit her with overwhelming force, and she smiled.

'All gone,' Joel assured her. 'Our Mr Saloman looked exhausted.'

'And our Mr Hanson looked bewildered,' she laughed. 'He doesn't seem to know much about shopping for groceries. I'll bet his wife knows more than he does.' She gave a sigh of relief as she slipped off her shoes. The appearance of the two executives, right in the middle of her honeymoon day, had disturbed the order of things, and she hardly knew how to steer life back on to its proper course. It had been quickly apparent to her that husbands were not to be commanded here and there at will!

'Now that's an idea,' Joel said thoughtfully. 'A committee of wives to shop for quality control? I might take that up with the board after I get them moved.'

'Moved?'

'Yes,' said Joel firmly. 'We're moving the corporate headquarters to Laconia. I like it up here.'

'So do I,' Maddie said softly as she settled back against the soft cushion. 'And you say Dr Burton gave you some information?'

'Well, not exactly.' Joel seemed to be having some trouble with his eyes. They kept flitting away from contact with her. 'I got the information second-hand, so to speak. Your aunt has made a remarkable recovery, and will be home tomorrow!'

'Why, that's wonderful news,' Maddie said doubtfully. 'You're sure? One of the nurses told you?'

'I guess you could say that.' It was an evasion, but she was too wrapped up in her new role as Mrs Fairmont to question him. Besides, she wanted to maintain the cloud of euphoria in which she lived at the moment.

'Then I'll go in tonight during the regular visiting hours and bring her some coming-home clothes,' she said firmly, and was surprised to see her new husband almost choke to death.

'I don't think that would be wise,' he gobbled as he struggled for breath. 'Your aunt needs her sleep, you know. I don't think Dr Burton would encourage any further visits. And your uncle Fred will see that she gets home tomorrow.'

Madeleine rubbed her eyes. Sleep had been in short supply the night before, and then all morning she had ridden the peaks of emotion with Tante Marie. Added to it all, the shock of her own wedding had worn her out. But with all the good news about Tante, she felt a large burden lifting from her shoulders, and knew she could rest peacefully for the first night in some time. 'I'm going up to bed,' she said, yawning. 'Goodnight.'

Joel watched as she got up, stretched, and headed for the stairs. 'Goodnight,' he called after her. She missed the wry smile on his face as he got up and covered Bluebeard's cage, effectively sending the bird off to sleep.

Maddie went through her usual procedures by rote, her mind busy on other things. She brushed her teeth, wasted time on combing her hair, scrubbed her face clean of the little make-up she usually used, and slipped into her old nightgown before padding down the hall into her bedroom. Mehitabel was stretched out at the foot of the bed. Maddie patted the cat's raised head and gently scratched behind his ears. 'Tante's coming home tomorrow,' she whispered. The animal purred approvingly and curled up into a ball.

There were vague thoughts wandering through Maddie's head. Facts, hard-to-identify facts, kept sliding in and out of focus, and she was unable to penetrate the mystery. She sat on the edge of her bed, thinking, then gave it all up as not worthwhile. Surely, in the morning, when she and the day were both brighter, things would clear up? Nodding her head, she discarded her slippers and slipped under the sheet that was her only summertime cover.

But sleep eluded her. She snapped on her bedside light and picked up the novel she had been reading for a week. Noises penetrated as the old house settled for the night. She laid the book down on her stomach and listened. Pipes were gurgling in the adjacent bathroom. Footsteps thumped down the hall. And her door flew open.

'Good lord, what are you doing in my bedroom?' She sat up with a jerk as the tall shadow moved into the circle of the bedlamp. 'Joel?'

'Well, I *am* your husband,' he said drily as he stepped out of his slippers and moved a hand towards the belt that held his robe in place.

'Oh, my!' Maddie slid down again in the bed, pulling the sheet up to her neck. 'I—I think I forgot about *that* part of being married!'

'I know. I didn't. Are you trying to tell me you don't want to?'

'I—no.' Her fingers ravelled at the hemline of the sheet, twisting nervous little knots into the fabric. 'No, I wouldn't dream of doing that.' And then she added plaintively, 'How could I have forgotten?'

'Freudian slip,' he laughed. Excitement was building up in Maddie's always sensible head. She tingled from head to toe just from seeing him. This was different from the night on the island. She was no longer driven by terror, haunted by fears. Now her only haunting was anticipation.

'I—don't know much about this,' she said breathlessly. 'Only what I've seen on television.'

Joel reached down to the foot of the bed and picked the cat up by the scruff of his neck. 'Now that's something I can't stand,' he said cheerfully as he walked over to the door and deposited the insulted cat in the hall. And closed the door behind him.

'You look so very——' Maddie murmured hesitantly as he came back to the side of the bed.

'All the better to eat you with,' he laughed. His hand moved at the belt. The terrycloth robe slipped off his shoulders and fell to the floor. The bedlamp was close to him. The golden circle of light painted his form clearly. Like a Greek god, Maddie thought.

'I——' she started to say, then winced as the bed sank under his weight. In a moment he was stretched out on his back, a few inches away from her, hands clasped behind his head.

'I—really don't——' she started to say, then lost control of her voice as his hand gently touched her throat, and trailed a line of fire down between her breasts.

'You really do,' he laughed. 'No more conversation. There's work at hand.'

Madeleine Charbonneau had spent a lifetime under instruction, building up a huge sea-wall in her mind. On her side was civilisation, order, calm. On the other was the restless tide, trying to break down the wall. Now, suddenly, wall-maintenance was no longer of interest to her. The seas of change rolled over her, and she totally abandoned all her learned patterns.

It was the warmth of him, lying there beside her, totally naked. It was the movement of his hands as they coursed lightly up and down her shivering frame. Somehow, without her knowledge, the hem of her nightgown was up at her neck. She *knew* how it got over her head. She helped.

Some fool female voice was muttering, 'Oh, my,' over and over again as Joel's lips captured the bronze peak of her breast. Sensation became fever as he sipped the sweetness of her. Her hand tangled in his hair and her hips rolled as he transferred to her other breast.

His hand wandered. Down the soft line of her stomach, and over the edge. And all Maddie could do was squirm in the ecstasy of it all. Time became elongated. Seconds felt like hours, and the pressure built. Nor was she the only one involved; Joel was panting, as if he were running a race. Perspiration stood on his forehead as his tongue chased a trail up from her breast to her neck, and then to the tip of her ear, before returning to the hardened cone of her nipple.

It was all panic, emotion, explosion; but only anticipatory. She knew it somehow, and wanted more, but did not know what to do about it. For some reason her eyes were glued shut, as if being walled in with these new emotions would make them last the longer.

And finally, when she was about to burst, Joel shifted his weight and rolled over on top of her. His busy tongue advanced to her mouth. She returned kiss for kiss, hugging him as if her life depended on it. Her legs parted at the urging of one of his knees, and for just a second he was still.

'Don't,' she muttered feverishly.

'Don't?'

'Don't stop,' Maddie sighed, and tried rocking her hips to force him back into action.

'Yes,' he muttered. She could feel the prodding as he sought for entry, the gentle stroking as he advanced a millimetre at a time, the pause when he reached the obstruction, and then the massive surge as he drove deeply inside her.

There was a pain—slight, and of short duration, followed by climactic feelings of change. Wild smashing emotions. Nothing ladylike was involved. He had touched the primordial core within her, and she battered at him as fiercely as he battered at her. The war had become abruptly two-sided as they drove each other up and up to climax.

And then the slow falling off. The contentment. The sudden realisation that their bodies were covered with perspiration, that they were both panting, aching for breath. The memory of what they had achieved together. 'Oh, my,' Maddie muttered, tasting blood in her mouth from where she had bitten a lip.

A long moment of comfort, with his weight balanced on her broad hips, and the quiet contact before he rolled to one side, pulled her up into the circle of his arms, and kissed the forehead that nestled against his shoulder. 'Well!' he said. 'A twenty-seven-year-old virgin!' And a self-satisfied sigh of contentment followed.

'Did I—did I do all right?' she asked hesitantly, squirming around to look up at him.

'Lady,' he laughed, 'if that's what you learned from television I'm going to have to watch that channel!'

'Well, I don't have anything to compare it to,' she said in a very subdued tone.

'I know that,' he assured her. 'Loving you is as easy as falling off a log, young lady!'

'I—oh, my,' Maddie sighed. 'Love? I'm happy you feel that way!' And if the *two* of us love, how could anything go wrong, her conscience comforted her!

'Believe,' he chuckled, and patted her bottom. 'Want something to drink? I get terribly thirsty on occasions like this.'

'Me too. I mean—yes, I'd like something to drink. Want me to get it?'

'Don't be silly. You stay right there and recoup your strength. The evening is still young yet!'

Morning came bright and early, and Maddie paid not the slightest bit of attention to it. Her husband had kept her awake until late into the night, and then, when he woke up before sunrise, had demonstrated his technique again. And only then had she dropped off into a warm, satisfied dream, in which he played a very great part indeed.

So when the doorbell went at about nine o'clock, and there seemed to be nobody around to answer, Maddie came fully awake with a start. Her nightgown had disappeared under the tangle of pillows and sheets. She hunted for it—until the bell chimed again—before she gave up and slipped into her robe.

The hall stairs were cold to her bare feet, but the bell rang for a third time, Bluebeard squawked in the distance, and Mehitabel howled. So by the time Maddie reached the door, totally dishevelled, Uncle Fred's police cruiser was backing out of the drive, and Tante Marie was standing on the doorstep.

Madeleine fumbled for the dead bolt lock and the retaining chain, and managed to get the door open. 'Oh, Tante!' She hugged the tiny woman until her aunt protested mildly.

'—before you squeeze me to death,' the old lady was saying when Maddie realised what her own strength was doing.

'Come in, come in,' Maddie exclaimed excitedly. 'It's so hard to believe! Yesterday you were—at death's door and I was single. And now you're up and about, and—so am I. Come in, love!'

'At death's door? I don't remember that part.' Tante made her way directly to the kitchen and sank down to rest at the table. 'Tea,' she commanded. 'They don't know how to make tea at that hospital. Or anything else fit to eat, for that matter!' The old lady was doing her best to be cheerful, hiding her tiredness behind a smile.

'Oh, Tante!' Maddie leaned both elbows on the table as she watched her elderly relative sip at the hot liquid. 'I—I've missed you so much.'

'I doubt it,' Tante observed with a twinkle in her eye. 'As I remember my wedding night—I could have forgotten the world!'

'But——' Maddie stuttered, 'I didn't even know you were married!'

'No reason why you should,' the old lady returned. A gentle smile played at the corners of her mouth. 'It was long before your time, my dear. Charlie was just twenty—and drafted for the War. The Great War, you know. World War One. Our parents objected, but we were married a week before his unit sailed to France.'

She stared into her teacup as if reading her fortune in it.

'So many names and places. We thought no one would ever forget—but they have, haven't they? Belleau Wood, the Somme, Château Thierry? Charlie was there. He never came back.'

One dainty hand stabbed at a tear, and then Tante Marie had put it all behind her. 'But you? Where is your husband? What about your honeymoon?'

Maddie smiled at the title. My husband! If I'm not careful I'll really flip, she warned herself. God didn't invent men just specifically for me! 'He left me a note,' she admitted. 'He thought—he didn't want to be here when you came home, because he thought that would spoil our time together. Can you imagine that? And we're postponing the honeymoon until you get better, Tante.'

There was a certain suspicious look in her aunt's eyes, but Madeleine was too deep in her own miracles to notice, or even hear the dry tone as Tante Marie said, 'No, I can't imagine that.'

'Joel had to go down to Massachusetts for the day,' Maddie rattled on. 'He wrote something about shaking things up at the warehouse in Worcester. He'll be back tonight. By helicopter, would you believe that? You were right, Tante. It *is* just as easy to love a rich man as a poor one. And I thought I was going to support him while he got his book written. Hah!'

'So you finally found out,' her aunt mused.

'And that's not all I found out,' Maddie added. Her great-aunt looked at her apprehensively.

'I think I'm tired. I really ought to take a nap,' the old lady said. 'You *do* understand, my dear?'

'Of course I do,' Maddie returned. 'Let me help you.'

A good hour was required, settling her great-aunt into her own nightgown, and her own bed, but by the time Maddie tiptoed over to pull the shades at the windows the old lady was fast asleep. She looked healthier than she ever had, Maddie thought as she went back downstairs.

There were things to be done. More than fifty people had tramped through the house yesterday offering congratulations. Crumbs and crusts and dirty glasses littered the floor. It took half an hour just to assemble the dirty dishes and cutlery in the kitchen, and another hour to vacuum thoroughly.

By noon she had finished. The kitchen gleamed, the house sparkled, and Tante Marie slept through it all. Maddie went up twice to peep. The old lady was resting comfortably, turned on her side with a satisfied expression on her face.

Across the hall, in what once had been Maddie's private room, she faced the hodge-podge of sharing, and laughed so hard she collapsed on the bed. His and hers, Joel and Madeleine! His consisted of a suit, scattered in various places across the room. The trousers were the same ones he had worn on Glory Island, crumpled, water-stained, and discarded. Now, a good wife would get that whole suit together, she told herself, and get it cleaned. Right?

It was a labour of love. She brought up his suitcase, hanging the few items it contained in the closet. The matching jacket was not as dirty as the slacks, but, like her own suits, should be cleaned all at once. Smiling to herself, she emptied the pockets.

Old opened letters, notes to himself, change, handkerchiefs, it all cascaded out as she checked. Probably a dozen things he had forgotten; I wonder if a good wife ought to read his mail, Maddie teased herself. Why not? We are one, isn't that what the preacher said? But not now. She stuffed the mass of material, including the loose change, into the pocket of her apron. After all, he deserved to lose the money. Finders keepers, she told herself.

The big grin reflected from the mirror in front of her. Madeleine Fairmont, she acknowledged, and went happily downstairs. Her mind was full of the excitement of her bridal night as she walked out on to the back porch with a glass of iced tea in her hand. The ice cubes tinkled gently. Bluebeard's cage was hanging from *her* rafters, with a cloth over it.

Maddie climbed up on one of the chairs and removed the blinder. The parrot was instantly alive. 'About time,' he chortled. He added a couple of ear-shaking whistles. 'Kill the cat,' he added, and played dead, rolling over to hang upside down from his perch.

'You don't catch me twice with that one,' Maddie laughed at him as she opened his cage door and climbed down to enjoy her cool drink. The bird hopped down to the lintel of the open door and cocked his head, watching her with those beady eyes.

Across the way, by the other house, a shadow moved. Maddie shaded her eyes against the morning sun and peered out. A tall gaunt woman was walking slowly down to the fence. The woman paused there, a gloomy expression on her face. 'Mama!' the parrot squalled. He launched himself from the cage and flew clumsily across the lawn, circled the woman, and landed on her shoulder.

'Mama indeed,' muttered Maddie. '*Somebody* loves her, and she's my mother-in-law.' Action followed thought. In a moment she was striding across the lawn with two glasses of ice-cold tea in her hands. The woman had turned away, but when the parrot squawked again she stopped and waited.

'Mrs Fairmont!' Maddie called. 'I'm Maddie—Madeleine Charbonneau—I'm sorry, Madeleine Fairmont. Would you care for some tea?'

'I don't mind if I do.' Close up, Mrs Fairmont looked to be in her early fifties, neatly dressed, with remnants of past beauty sparking her cheeks. Her grey hair was neatly combed, and the grey dress she wore was neat—and expensive. She was not at all the battleaxe of yesterday at the hospital. 'So you married my son?

'Yes—I guess I did,' Maddie stammered. 'I hope you don't mind. He's gone off to work this morning.'

'He's gone off to what?' The older woman had a delightful smile, Maddie thought.

'To work,' she repeated. 'I don't understand it all. Yesterday we had a couple of visitors from the Corporation Headquarters, and today Joel's gone to Worcester. He said something about a shake-up at the distribution centre.'

'So he really *is* doing something useful!' The elder Mrs Fairmont's eyes sparkled. 'And you're responsible for all this? Lord, for years I've been trying to get him to—take control of things. Well, young lady, I guess I've made a mistake about you. Is it too late to welcome you to the family?'

'Not at all,' Maddie laughed as she leaned over the fence. The cheek she kissed was soft, the eyes that were so close had a tear in them, and Maddie realised that she had a great deal to discuss with that husband of hers concerning his mother!

'Why don't you come down to the house and meet my aunt Marie?' she invited, throwing caution to the

winds. 'All you have to do is to walk around to the front
of the house and go around the fence.'

Mrs Fairmont looked at the solidly-constructed barrier
between them, and shook her head. 'No, I don't think
so. My son put up the fence and then moved to the opposite side. It seems to me there's a message there. I've
no further intention of interfering with his life. I do hope
you'll be happy with him, Madeleine.'

'Please—call me Maddie,' she interrupted. 'Everyone
does except when they're angry with me.'

'All right—Maddie. But let me warn you. Don't let
him get away with anything, or he'll run all over you!
Get along now, Bluebeard.' She enticed the parrot on to
her finger and handed him back over the fence, where
he jumped to Maddie's shoulder, squawked a couple of
times in her ear, and settled down.

While the two women were talking neither had observed Mehitabel, slinking belly-deep in the grass until
he was only a foot or so away. The cat measured his
advantages, vaulted up on to the top rail of the fence,
and from there, in one graceful non-stop bound, directly towards the bird on Maddie's shoulder.

But Bluebeard had not got his name for nothing. The
wily old bird, with forty years of experience behind him,
fluttered straight up in the air and came back down on
the cat's back, beak down, nipping. Mehitabel dug his
claws into Maddie's shirt and screamed a banshee wail
of surprise and defeat before he abandoned the unequal
struggle and ran for the house. The bird circled above
his head, making dive-bombing approaches to spur the
cat on.

Maddie forgot what she had planned to say under the
combined assault. Mrs Fairmont laughed. 'Bluebeard
will take only so much harassment from a cat before he

puts it in its place, Maddie. There won't be any more trouble between that pair.'

'You *do* intend to stay in Laconia for a while, Mrs Fairmont?'

'I don't know, Maddie,' the other woman replied sadly. 'I had hoped to talk to my son. Really talk—get to know Joel, something neither of us has ever tried to do before. But the way things are——'

'Things could get better,' Madeleine maintained stoutly. 'I *know* things will get better. Stay at least another day or two?'

'If you insist, child. It will be difficult. I haven't been able to recruit a maid or a cook, and it's been a long time since I've had to look after myself—but for a day or two, yes.' Mrs Fairmont paused, deep in thought. 'Madeleine—what a lovely name,' she continued. 'Someone told me you'd lost your father and mother, both. You must call me Mother!' Madeleine smiled, as sunny as the heavens, and turned back towards the house to rescue Mehitabel, who was hiding under the lip of the veranda and sharing his anguish with the world.

Tante Marie was up and dressed and on the telephone when Madeleine came in. 'I never could sleep in the daytime,' the old lady said, disregarding the fact that she had already slept for more than four hours. 'I'm getting a few of my friends together, Maddie. Do you suppose you could whip up something?'

'Of course I could,' she promised, and went over to kiss her relative. Her great-aunt was surprised. The two had grown older together, and shared love together, but kissing was not one of the things encouraged in the staid household.

Maddie, who thought she could read her aunt's mind with a great deal of ease, went out to the kitchen to get with the project. By two o'clock the bridge club had clattered in, Maddie's tea and finger sandwiches had all been devoured, and Mrs Mahoney had said, 'My, how you've grown, Madeleine! And married? I don't believe it!'

And I feel the same way, Maddie told herself as she went back to the porch and huddled in the swing with a cool glass of iced tea in her hand. *I don't believe it myself! He's been away for six hours already! How could I ever have believed I hated him?*

The front door bell broke in on her thoughts. Bluebeard squawked. 'I'm going, I'm going,' Maddie muttered as she pattered across the floor in bare feet. The regular mailman waited outside patiently.

'Special delivery,' Mr Palack announced. 'Have to sign here, Maddie.' He had been delivering on that route for the past fifteen years, and he recognised a bride when he saw one. He whistled as he went down the steps, leaving her with a handful of envelopes and half a dozen advertising circulars. She weighed them in one hand, then scuttled back to the porch and sat down.

A slight movement, and the crackle that originated in her pocket called to mind the letters she had purloined from her husband's jacket, and reminded her that she had to call the cleaners. But the letters intrigued. 'Nosey Fairmont,' she chided herself, then spread Joel's material out on the couch beside her own mail.

She sipped at her iced tea and settled back for a moment. Mehitabel was coiled up on the top step, still nursing his bent ego. Bluebeard had settled into his cage, resting on the little trapeze bar, and occasionally making little whistling noises. *All's right with my world,* Maddie told herself.

The special delivery item was a small problem. An overdue light bill, with a flashy red 'Second Warning'

stamped over its heading. And Maddie had not a cent
left in the bank until Henri paid off her last commissions. She tapped the notice against her fingernail,
absorbing but not hearing the conversation from the
bridge group, until Mrs McCafferty, who had an un-
usually shrill voice, said, '—and if it's a bill, I leave it
for my husband!'

'Like St Michael with guidance directly from Heaven,'
muttered Maddie. 'The very thing! I'll leave it for my
husband!'

'Hot patootie!' the parrot screamed at her. 'Now ya
got it, babe!'

Maddie smiled up at the bird. 'I'm learning, I'm
learning,' she called. 'Give me time!' The bird whistled
an agreement as she reached for the second envelope
without looking at the addressee. Another bill.

She unfolded it carefully. It was a dun from Gunstock
Lodge, the ski-resort on the mountain of the same name.
'For overtime special housekeeping job on Glory Island,'
it said, and quoted a sizeable fee. Probably a thing he's
started already for the conference centre, she decided,
and laid it aside. But something caught her eye and then
eluded her. She picked up the bill again and studied it.
Nothing had changed. It seemed all legal and above
board.

Until she looked for the third time at the billhead.
The date shown for the service provided was the fourteenth of August, two days *before* she and Joel had spent
the night at the Murchison manor. Maddie's thinking
processes came to a thumping halt. She thumbed the
paper, then flipped it over to read the ingredients.
Sleeping bag (1), duvet (1), wine (1 case), candles (6),
lanterns (2), sundries (4), one half-cord chopped wood.

Facts accumulated plus facts analysed equal something rotten in the state of Denmark, her calculating mind

told her! Two days *before* we go to the island he contracts for all this stuff, on an island he's never heard of before? Very thoughtful now, she put the bill aside carefully and turned to the next envelope.

Another bill. Frasher Seaplane Service, asking for an astronomical amount for: 'Air evacuation two persons from Glory Island 15 August. Special instructions: be outside Peddle Cove at dawn, 17 August. Do not, repeat, do not approach *over* island area. In case of difficulties, contact Mr Joel Fairmont, Laconia telephone 555 6505!' Maddie turned the bond-marked paper over a couple of times, then checked again. 'Telephone order of 14 August,' the final note added.

The third item was a carefully folded single sheet of embossed paper, enclosed in an expensive envelope. She slipped the paper out, apprehensive, but unwilling to turn back. 'City of Laconia,' the ornate heading read. A marriage licence with her name on it—and in the upper right-hand corner, the date of issue. The thirteenth of August!

Very suddenly Madeleine Fairmont realised that it had become a dark day indeed! She crumpled up all her evidence and crammed it into her pocket. Inside the house the ladies of the bridge club were making going-away noises. Maddie stood up and stretched as she thought, her mind probing at the whole train of events that had led up to that fateful day. She was pacing the porch when the front door slammed and a cheery voice called, 'Maddie? I'm home!'

Don't let him get away with anything! Her mother-in-law's voice echoed in her ear. Joel Fairmont, schemer *extraordinaire*! He had stocked the old Murchison house with sleeping gear two days *before* they required it. And made arrangements for an air-rescue for the day after. All this accomplished even *before* the storm. The storm, and Tante Marie's illness? I'll bet *that* shook him up. But see how skilfully he weaved it all into the plot? Tante's on her deathbed, Madeleine! So we *have* to get married right away, right! That arrogant, arrant man! Nothing's changed! He's the man I love to hate. So I'll have it out with the monster, and then I'll file for an annulment!

'You will over my dead body,' she argued under her breath. 'Why bite off my own nose to spite my face? He's a good man, and, at twenty-seven a girl doesn't get all that many chances. But if I let him get away with it, there'll be no controlling him! Somebody's going to suffer, and that's a fact!'

She took another moment to arrange her face in a carefully neutral shade of suppressed anger, then strode into the living room. The guilty rascal was standing beside Tante Marie, deep in conversation—which broke off the instant Maddie came across the threshold.

'There you are, darling,' Joel beamed as he came across the room and tried to kiss her. She evaded his grip, and glared at him. The coolness could not be gainsaid.

'Oh, my,' her aunt said vaguely as she sank into the nearest chair.

'I—er—have you had a good day?' Joel asked cautiously.

'I think I need to have a talk with both of you,' Maddie announced grimly, tapping the crumpled envelopes with her fingernail.

CHAPTER TEN

TANTE MARIE settled back in her special chair, her feet up on the hassock sporting her own gros-point design, and sipped at the tea which Maddie had brought. 'Now, dear, what's the problem?'

'I think I need to gather a little more evidence,' Madeleine said, from her standing position in the middle of the floor.

'Well, I——' Joel started to say.

'Hush!' she commanded. 'Now, Tante, exactly why did you go into the hospital?'

Her aunt cocked her head. Almost exactly like Bluebeard, Maddie thought madly. 'Why, you must have forgotten,' Tante said in her soft, gentle voice. 'Don't you remember? Dr Burton said I ought to have a yearly check-up, and the best thing to do would be to go into hospital for the two days each year so they could run all those tests and things.'

'Good God!' Maddie paced the floor, thinking furiously as she took two steps one way, two the other. 'It's all so simple. And Tuesday and Wednesday were the days we had reserved.' Her aunt nodded happily, and finished off her tea.

'Would you believe it, Tante,' Maddie continued grimly. 'We've fallen into the hands of one of the prime con-men of Western civilisation!'

'Oh, I wouldn't say that,' the old lady responded softly. 'It was—a little startling, to begin with, there in the hospital, when you and Joel burst in. But then it wasn't too hard to see what was going on, and I didn't quite have the—gall—to interfere.' She settled back in her chair, the perfect example of innocent dignity. 'Besides, you know how much I wanted to see you married.'

'My own aunt!' gasped Maddie. 'My very own aunt!'

'Great-aunt,' Tante admonished with dignity. 'That's a different position entirely. One generation further removed, and deserving just that much more respect. Now then——' she struggled to her feet and gave them both a wide grin '—since I'm a strong believer in the idea that matrimony can't be shared among three, I'll just go along and let you two fight——'

'Discuss,' Maddie interrupted.

'Yes, of course,' her aunt replied. 'Discuss—whatever it is you have to discuss. I understand that Joel's mother is living next door. I believe I'll walk up there and have a few words with her.'

'Go carefully,' Maddie warned. 'That fool fence is in everyone's way. And it may take some time to give this— man—a fair trial!'

'Fair trial, hah!' snorted Joel as he sank back on the sofa. 'Guilty until proved innocent, is that not the way?' His deep blue eyes threatened thunder as he banged the arm of his seat, then winced as if his hand hurt. Tante Marie swept out of the room with more speed than one would expect from a woman fresh out of the hospital.

'You're my wife,' he continued. 'You don't have jurisdiction. A husband can't be made to testify against his will!'

'You'd better be willing, you scoundrel,' Maddie threatened through clenched teeth. 'You've pulled the wool completely over our eyes!'

'Now you're blaming me for your own faults,' he told her coolly. 'There are none so blind as those who won't see!'

'Now that's just enough!' snapped Maddie. 'Pay attention. I have the floor!'

'Yes, and it didn't get cleaned very well today,' Joel sniffed. 'You should spend more time with "clean" than with "confrontation". And have a little respect for my position. I'm the head of the household now.'

'Head?' Maddie shouted. 'Why, you—— In about twenty minutes I'm going to hand you your head in a basket!'

'With what am I charged?' Joel interrupted. Maddie walked over in front of him, and wished she hadn't. The closer she got to the man the weaker her determination grew. She searched her mind madly.

'Conspiracy to commit marriage by fraud,' she announced solemnly. He reached up and brushed the lock of hair out of his eyes, leaving her aching to do exactly the same thing. Get a grip on yourself, she raged, or you'll end up a doormat for the rest of your life!

'You, Joel Fairmont, do you recall the fourteenth of August?'

'Can't say that I do,' he replied. 'Is it Bluebeard's birthday or something?'

'It was two days *before* we went to Glory Island,' Maddie reminded him desperately, trying to keep control of the situation. 'On that afternoon or night, Joel Fairmont, did you not make arrangements with the caterer at Gunstock Lodge to provide sleeping bags and quilts and wine and wood—and other things—in the Murchison house?'

He hesitated for a moment, gauging her temper. 'And if I said I didn't?'

'I have the bill here,' she shouted at him as she ripped the paper from her pocket, tearing it in half.

'Reading my mail already? I thought newlyweds had at least a few weeks of mutual trust!'

'Don't beat around the bush,' grumbled Maddie. 'Answer the question.'

'I was only asking. So I won't say that.'

'Then you admit that you did it?'

'Yes, I admit it. What happened to that sweet, loving girl I married? I don't know that I care for the shrew in front of me! Surely you wouldn't have wanted to spend a night in that house without any comforts!'

'Just answer the questions, wise guy,' she muttered. 'Isn't it also true that the airplane rescue was no rescue at all? Didn't you arrange earlier for that man to come to get us?'

'I did.' Joel grinned at her, as if daring her to make something out of it. 'I thought that was just the right touch—at the time. Now that I reflect, perhaps it was a mistake.'

'Then that whole thing was a frame-up!' she shouted as she paced back and forth in front of him.

'Not the *whole* thing,' Joel reflected judiciously. 'The storm was no part of my plan at all.' He pursed his lips in and out a couple of times, thinking. 'And losing Henri's boat wasn't part of the original scheme either—but it provided the frosting on the cake, didn't it!'

She allowed the bait to distract her. 'You enjoyed hurting Henri, didn't you?' she hissed. 'You were *glad* that his boat was wrecked! And he never did a single bad thing to you!'

'Of course he did,' he returned. 'He was trying to steal my girl. Nobody in his right mind is going to put up with that!'

'I——' she stuttered as her temper took control.

'Now, Madeleine, don't stutter,' he cautioned warily. 'It always happens when you lose your temper.'

'I'm not mad,' Maddie snarled, 'I'm just—mad! You sit there looking as if butter wouldn't melt in your mouth, when all the time you've been running the biggest scam in New Hampshire. You took me to Glory Island——'

'Let's be entirely fair about this,' he said, shifting his position on the sofa. Maddie backed away, not sure what might happen next. 'As I recollect, *you* took *me*!'

'I don't care!' she screamed. Out on the porch, aroused by the noise, Bluebeard hopped out of his cage and squawked, 'Abandon ship, mates. Pretty baby!'

'You, Joel Fairmont, you took me out to Glory purposely to ruin my reputation, didn't you!'

'I guess that's right,' he agreed amiably. 'It seemed like such a good idea at the time.' He nodded to emphasise the fact. 'Every last bit. I took you out to the island to compromise you, and I took advantage of your aunt's illness to get you to marry me. How else do you think I could have done it? You have a terrible reputation for backing off at the last minute. If I'd tried to propose to you in the normal way you'd still be running, Madeleine Fairmont. Your aunt told me all about your little habits. And now just what are we getting at?'

'What I'm getting at is that I've been railroaded by as smooth a con-person as ever the world has seen!' Maddie's voice softened as she came to a halt directly in front of him. 'And I'm not finished with the interrogation yet. The marriage licence. What about the mar-

riage licence that you just *happened* to have in your
pocket when we went to the hospital! The one that you
applied for several days *before* we went to Glory? What
about that?'

'Maybe it's just a habit with me,' Joel suggested cautiously. 'Maybe I carry a blank one around with me, and
just fill in the name at the proper time?'

'Don't give me that,' she snapped. 'It has to be all
filled in in front of the clerk! You took advantage of
me, Joel Fairmont, and now Tante Marie will be
expecting—children around the house and——'

'Are you telling me that you don't want to be married
to me?' her husband asked.

'I—no,' she answered, startled. 'I mean—yes. Yes, I
do want to be married to you.'

'Then just because I arranged to smooth the way, why
are you protesting? Marriages have always been arranged, through the centuries!' Joel nodded sagely, then
a sorrowful expression came over his face. 'I feel very
badly about having to trick you, Maddie. But I hope
you don't have second thoughts. I hate the idea of divorce, and we're too far down the Pike for an annulment.'

'I do too.' Maddie put both hands on her hips and
glared at him. 'Hate divorce, I mean. I don't intend to
divorce you. I might murder you, but no divorce. You're
not getting off *that* easy, believe me!'

'And now that we've settled the only important point,
how about including me in the general amnesty,
Maddie?' He was inches away from her, having risen
from the couch with supple grace. She had no intention
of letting him off the hook that easily, and at the same
time she knew that another minute in close proximity
would bring all her intentions to naught.

'I—damn you! Do you expect me to share a house with you after that—trickery!' She whirled away from him and dashed out of the room so he could not see the tears, crashed through the back screen door, and found herself hugging one of the porch pillars. The old bird watched her for a moment, then zoomed down to perch on her shoulder.

'Pretty baby,' the bird croaked, then added a very profound bit of wisdom. He shuffled closer to her ear, leaned his beak into it, and squawked, *'Don't get mad, get even!'*

'Wise bird,' Maddie whispered through her sniffles. 'Wise, wise bird. I shall *never* make soup out of you!'

'Darby McGraw,' the bird squawked. 'Bring aft the rum, Darby!' Maddie worked up a smile for him, and walked quietly over to the window and looked in. Joel was sitting at table in the kitchen, playing games with his coffee mug. Mr Fairmont could perhaps be said not to be enjoying life at that particular moment. With a little grimace Maddie climbed down from the porch and headed for the adjacent house.

'Well, it took you long enough,' said Joel as Maddie came in at the back door just as dusk was settling in.

'Yes,' she said quietly as she walked over to the sink and scrubbed her hands enthusiastically. 'I forgot it was *my* house I was running away from.'

'You and I need to have a few dozen more words,' he growled. 'I don't intend there to be any question about who wears the pants in this family!'

'Of course, Joel,' she said sweetly. He ran a nervous hand through his hair and glared at her as if expecting a riot.

'All right,' he said, exasperated. 'I know something's going on. What is it now?'

'Why, nothing.' She turned to dry her hands on the kitchen towel. 'Nothing's going on. You said there was to be no question about who wears the pants——'

'Me,' he snapped. 'That's who. Me!'

'Yes, dear.' Maddie came over to the table and sat down across from him. 'I have it on good authority that you were a rotten child, Joel.' The statement lay flat on the table between them like an M-80 firecracker, lit and ready to blow.

Joel scowled at her. 'My mother,' he groaned. 'You've been talking to my mother!' Maddie nodded agreement.

'She's spent hours poisoning you against me. She hates me! God, I wish she hadn't come up here. I can't think of anything worse in the world than to have my mother live next door to me! Nothing!'

'She speaks well of you,' Maddie replied. 'Except that—well, you certainly had a lot of bad habits!'

His face was flushed as he came to her, putting a hand on each of her shoulders, and administering a little shake. 'Just why the hell,' he muttered angrily, 'do you think I went to all this trouble to marry you? Why?'

'What a good question,' she returned sarcastically. 'For my money? I don't have any.' The remark earned her a couple more shakes that set her teeth rattling.

'Listen carefully,' he growled. 'I married you because I love you.'

And there was the word, Maddie thought in awe. *I love you*. No matter how many arguments, how many conniving actions, those words put paid to all her doubts and all her travail. I married you because I love you, he had said! And so did I, Joel, she cried to herself. So did

I. And now what? Forgiveness overflowing into the
stream of life? Let the scoundrel—no, that's the wrong
word—the rascal get away with all this? Never happen!
He deserves just a *tiny* bit of flaying, for his conscience's
sake!

'If you say so, Joel.' She began collecting dirty dishes.
He snatched one of her wrists and pulled her back in
front of him.

'None of that,' he told her. 'I didn't get you to be a
kitchen drudge.'

'Oh?' She looked up at him, managing to keep her
face in neutral. Not one hint of a smile, or the whole
game would be up.

'I know you're spilling over with plans for vengeance,' he muttered as he took both her hands in his.
'But you listen, lady! I fell in love with you that first
night, standing on my back porch, when you came
barging up the stairs looking for Joel Fairmont! You
knocked me over in more ways than one! Do you remember that?'

Do I? Her heart skipped a beat. The same night I fell
in love with him! And then I let his—arrogance—put
me off. Look how much time we've wasted! She stared
up at him with love shining in her eyes.

Bluebeard, disturbed by all the movement, fluttered
off her shoulder and on to his favourite perch on top of
the refrigerator.

'I've had a number of talks with Tante Marie,' Joel
continued roughly. 'Always your pattern with men has
been the same. You fall in love with some yokel, work
your way up to an engagement, then run for the hills.
Well, I wasn't about to let you get away with that, young
lady. So I purposely set out on a campaign to aggravate

you enough to throw you off balance. All your aunt's idea. A fine lady, that one!'

'My own—my very own aunt?' Maddie stammered.

'Your very own,' he laughed. 'Except for the fiasco at Glory Island. That was all my own idea! And I *did* leave your aunt a note! Is it *my* fault the storm came up and blew my plans to a fare-thee-well?'

'Oh, my!' she sighed, and very firmly clamped her lips together and ducked her head.

'Come on, upstairs.' He pulled at her wrist. Maddie set the plates back down on the table and allowed him to tow her up the stairs and into their bedroom. 'Lie down there,' he said seriously, 'I want to talk to you.'

'Talk?' The grin escaped her control. The sight of the bed, looming there in the light of the tiny table lamp, had set off explosions she could hardly contain. Yesterday was yesterday was yesterday, she thought, and today is *bound* to be better.

'I want you to stop wearing these knit sweaters,' he complained as his hand tugged at the front of the offending material, at the neck.

'Oh?' It was getting more and more difficult to hold in. Maddie, barely in control, pinched herself to offset the steadily building fires within.

'Yeah,' he grunted. 'No amount of ripping can get the damn things off!'

'But——' she started to say, but too late. The sweater was one of her favourites, a form-clinging light wool, which buttoned down the back. He was right, of course. The wool was too elastic.

'Bodice-ripping?' she asked faintly.

'Damn well right,' he said moodily, busy at his impossible task. 'This week I intend to spend time on

bodice-ripping research. Next week I'm going to devote
a day to my novel. I'll finish it——' Whatever he meant
to say went by the boards. Even his strength could not
rip the wool, but the buttons were another matter. Past
their pressure point, one after another they popped off
until finally the sweater came away in his hands—and
Maddie was wearing nothing underneath.

'Oh, lord!' he sighed, almost as if it were a prayer.
'Lie down here, lady.' He was already breathing hard,
and his excitement added to her own. She offered him
a Mona Lisa smile and lay back on the bed while he
struggled with shirt and tie and shoes and belt and——

'Oh, my,' Maddie said in true respect as she watched
him. With two quick wriggles she kicked her shoes off
and her skirt followed.

'Maddie,' he whispered hoarsely as he came down on
her in his urgent need. There was none of the gentleness
of the prior night. None of the long silences, and tender
awakenings. That could come later. At this one moment
the pair of them were aflame. She opened herself to his
thrusting, urging him on, moaning, tugging at his hair
to force him to hurry, swinging her hips until his hands
swept under her buttocks and locked her into position
as the target of his deepest thrust, and she screamed with
the joy of it as they both achieved a matching climax.

'Oh, my,' she muttered moments later. Joel was still
lying on top of her, his weight no problem at all, as they
regained their breath. She moved her hand, pushed back
that errant lock of hair off his forehead, used the palm
of her hand to dry the standing perspiration, then hugged
him eagerly.

'I love you so much,' she confessed. His grin was wide enough to fill the Grand Canyon.

'You'd better,' he chuckled, 'or I'll have to punish you again!'

'Was that what it was?' she laughed. He made a move to roll off, and she stopped him.

'Don't,' she sighed. 'I never knew anything could be so good. Stay there!'

Another moment of comfortable silence. 'If you were really angry at me,' she mused softly, 'do you think you could—punish me again?'

'I think so,' he laughed. 'Why should I get angry at you?'

'I heard it's not good to let husbands get away with everything they want,' she continued. 'Marriage is supposed to be a two-way street.'

'Of course. That's just what it is,' he said amiably. 'I love you too, sweetheart. You'll have to give up your real-estate job. I want you home.'

'That sounds—not very two-way,' she said. 'It sounds almost like an order.'

'I told you I was going to wear the pants in this family,' said Joel with pseudo-anger. 'And I intend to!'

'I don't mind that,' she whispered in his ear, then let the tip of her tongue explore. 'When you're wearing the pants you can be the boss of the world. But neither of us is wearing pants at the moment!'

'Rascal,' he muttered. 'What do you think you're doing?'

'Conducting a logical discussion,' she said solemnly, as her hands wandered up and down his back. 'Are we *really* married?'

He lifted his head and stared at her. 'What kind of a question is *that*?'

'I just wanted to be sure,' she sighed. 'Everything has happened so quickly that I had the suspicion it might only be a dream. But it's all real?'

'All real,' he chuckled in her ear. 'Good for a thousand years, or five million miles, which ever comes first.'

'Well, that's all right then,' she sighed. 'As long as it's legal. Go ahead—jump on me again.' Her sharp little teeth nibbled on his nearest ear, and her giggle was infectious.

'Oh, brother,' he sighed as he rolled half away from her, to lie on his side facing her. Her hand, which had been coursing across his buttocks, stayed in the same general area when he moved, and as a result ended up in a delicate position.

He responded with a quick intake of breath. 'Be careful of the family jewels,' he gasped. Her hand was still busy as Maddie looked over into his smiling face.

'Tell me about your mother,' she interjected. Surprise ran rampant over his face.

'With luck she'll go back to Boston today,' he murmured. 'I *know* I have to do something about that situation, but——'

'Then if you love me so much, you couldn't possibly be angry with me,' she pointed out. 'Especially since I've done something to help you in your new resolve. I invited your mother to come and live with us for the next four weeks. She's moving in tomorrow.'

'You what!' roared Joel as he pulled away from her, up to a sitting position. 'You what?'

'I invited your mother to come and live with us,' she repeated, a saucy smile playing across her face. 'And I ordered the fence company to come back tomorrow and take the fence down so we won't have to walk around it all the time. And what do you think of that, pantless Mr Fairmont!'

'Why, you mad little devil! You did that on purpose just to aggravate me!' The anger-furrows faded, and a deep-seated grin replaced them. 'Don't make so much noise,' he continued, tapping her gently on the tip of her nose. 'We wouldn't want to alarm Tante, would we? And besides, you now have both a husband and a parrot to satisfy!'

'Don't forget my cat, you monstrous——'

'Husband.' He supplied the word as one of his hands trapped her tingling breast.

'Husband,' he repeated. 'You know I'm going to have to punish you for all this nonsense?'

'Yes,' she smiled pertly. 'Two or three times—if you're capable of it!'

'I'll show you capable,' Joel laughed. And he did. Or rather—he tried!

Down on the porch in the moonlight Bluebeard the parrot squawked, 'Anchors aweigh. Pretty baby!' And Mehitabel, tired of playing games with stupid birds, started up McGrath Street looking for the Persian.

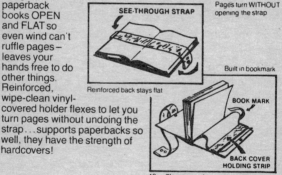

Especially for you, Christmas from
HARLEQUIN HISTORICALS

An enchanting collection of three Christmas stories by some of your favorite authors captures the spirit of the season in the 1800s

TUMBLEWEED CHRISTMAS by Kristin James

A "Bah, humbug" Texas rancher meets his match in his new housekeeper, a woman determined to bring the spirit of a Tumbleweed Christmas into his life—and love into his heart.

A CINDERELLA CHRISTMAS by Lucy Elliot

The perfect granddaughter, sister and aunt, Mary Hillyer seemed destined for spinsterhood until Jack Gates arrived to discover a woman with dreams and passions that were meant to be shared during a Cinderella Christmas.

**HOME FOR CHRISTMAS
by Heather Graham Pozzessere**

The magic of the season brings peace Home For Christmas when a Yankee captain and a Southern heiress fall in love during the Civil War.

Look for HARLEQUIN HISTORICALS CHRISTMAS STORIES in November wherever Harlequin books are sold.

HIST-XMAS-1

Indulge a Little, Give a Lot

To receive your free gift send us the required number of proofs-of-purchase from any specially marked "Indulge A Little" Harlequin or Silhouette book with the Offer Certificate properly completed, plus a cheque or money order (do not send cash) to cover postage and handling payable to Harlequin/Silhouette "Indulge A Little, Give A Lot" Offer. We will send you the specified gift.

Mail-in-Offer

OFFER CERTIFICATE

Item:	A. Collector's Doll	B. Soaps in a Basket	C. Potpourri Sachet	D. Scented Hangers
# of Proofs-of -Purchase	18	12	6	4
Postage & Handling	$3.25	$2.75	$2.25	$2.00
Check One				

Name _____

Address _____ Apt. # _____

City _____ State _____ Zip _____

ONE PROOF OF PURCHASE

To collect your free gift by mail you must include the necessary number of proofs-of-purchase plus postage and handling with offer certificate.

HP-1

Harlequin®/Silhouette®

Mail this certificate, designated number of proofs-of-purchase and check or money order for postage and handling to:

INDULGE A LITTLE
P.O. Box 9055 Buffalo, N.Y. 14269-9055

NOTE THIS IMPORTANT OFFER'S TERMS
Offer available in the United States and Canada.

Requests must be postmarked by February 28, 1990. Only proofs-of-purchase from specially marked "Indulge A Little" Harlequin or Silhouette books will be accepted. This certificate must accompany your request and may not be reproduced in any manner. Offer void where prohibited, taxed or restricted by law. LIMIT ONE GIFT PER NAME, FAMILY, GROUP, ORGANIZATION OR ADDRESS. Please allow up to 8 weeks after receipt of order for shipment. Offer good while quantities last. Collector's dolls will be mailed to first 15,000 qualifying submitters. All other submitters will receive 18 free previously unpublished Harlequin or Silhouette books and a postage and handling refund. For every specially marked book purchased during October, November and December, Harlequin/Silhouette will donate 5¢ to **Big Brothers/ Big Sisters Programs and Services** in the United States and Canada for a maximum contribution of $100,000.00.